Scandalous Pledge

Vi Carter

Contents

Blurb

Alex

My father controlled every move I made, even who I loved.

I've wanted Nadia since we were children, but a maid's daughter isn't fit for a Mafia king.

For nine years, I've protected her from the shadows, secretly dictating her every move--until now.

My father's death has set me free, and I will claim what is mine, even if it costs me an empire.

Nadia

I've loved him my whole life and have hated him for nearly a decade.

I would have given anything for Alex Murphy to make me his, but the day he pushed me aside changed everything.

Now he claims to want me for his wife, but he harbors secrets that could destroy everything.

Secrets that could cost me my life and his.

Will our love set us free or will his secrets keeps us apart?

Other Books by VI CARTER

MAFIA GAMES #3

MAFIA BOSS #4

MURPHY'S MAFIA MADE MEN

SINNER'S VOW #1

SAVAGE MARRIAGE #2

SCANDALOUS PLEDGE #3

CHAPTER ONE

NADIA

*T*HE RAIN IS SHARP. *As the sheets of water blow sideways, they hit the asphalt before bouncing back up. I should feel the cold. I should feel the heaviness of the rain. I should be running for cover. But I don't. I'm smiling; he's smiling, and at thirteen, I know this feeling I have for Alex Murphy is unstoppable.*

He's what makes me tick. He's like my batteries. Without him, nothing seems as bright, nothing seems possible, and nothing seems real.

His laughter dances around me, and as he advances closer, I see the shift in his gaze even before his laughter dies down, and he pushes his dark hair out of his eyes.

"You are a very bad influence on me." His height dwarfs everything around us. My heart does that funny dance that often shifts into when Alex looks at me differently than he normally does. It's at these moments when I'm at my freest that he looks at me differently. I want to tell him I only do these things, like running out into the rain, for his reaction. I'd jump off a cliff for his reaction.

His hand captures mine, and his warmth alerts the rest of my body to the drop in temperature. I slide closer, seeking his heat.

"If I jumped off a cliff, would you follow me?" I joke.

My mother always said that about me. 'If Alex Murphy jumped off a cliff, you would jump too.' I'd roll my eyes and tell her she was wrong.

She wasn't.

"How high of a cliff are we talking about?" Alex's dark eyes dance with mischief, and without words, I know he would. He would follow me across the cliff's edge and into whatever dark abyss lay below, and I know if we did jump into the unknown, we would be okay.

Alex dips his head, and I pucker my lips. I'm ready to taste the wolf. That's what I call him in my head. The lone wolf. He has brothers, but none of them are like Alex. No one is like Alex. He's one of a kind.

"Nadia Greenwood." My name being called smashes the memory. I nod at the man who holds the wooden door open for me. A pen is placed behind both his ears, and several fill his short-sleeved shirt's breast pocket.

The glossy magazine that had kept me occupied for a few minutes nearly slipped from my knee. I had forgotten about it as my brain decided we needed to revisit a ten-year-old memory over and over and over again.

I place the magazine on the mahogany table and do a quick sweep across the other three female candidates who are applying for the same job as me. I have the skills to be a receptionist, but if I was to base the outcome on all my other job interviews, I wasn't hopeful.

"Thank you." I take the door, relieving the man, who starts walking down a narrow hallway. On either side, phones ring in the large call center. Maybe I could work here in the office if I don't get the front desk. I mean, I'm a quick learner.

If I don't get the job—I want to pause that thought, but there is no pausing it—I would have to return to working for Alex Murphy.

God, I hate him. My feelings for him may still be unstoppable, but they have flipped on their head. Once, I loved him. I loved him so much and he fucking shattered my heart into a million pieces, and at the time, I would have allowed him to do it over and over again just to have a small piece of him.

At first, when he stopped hanging out with me, I couldn't function. I had a constant darkness that hung over me. It never left, but I found ways to deal with the gaping hole he left in my life.

"Mr. Jordan is waiting for you." The door is pushed open, and I step into a luxurious office. Mr. Jordan, who's a lot younger than I expected, stands up from behind a modern stainless steel desk with a wide white smile. He looks like someone I would love to work for. His warmth is immediate, even as his large hand engulfs mine.

"Miss Greenwood. Please take a seat," he says as he releases my hand.

I sit down and notice a shock of gray hair along the side of his head. Maybe he isn't as young as I first thought. Forties or early fifties. Either way, he looks friendly. He's a silver fox—that's what springs to mind. I spot several pictures on his desk, but I can't get a clear view of them.

He holds up my resume, and I put on my best smile each time he glances at me over it. My smart pencil skirt and white shirt fit me like a glove and only get worn for interviews. If my clothes could talk, I'd be rightfully screwed. If Mr. Jordan knew this was my twenty-second interview this year, he would give me my marching orders, thinking there was something wrong with me.

The sad part is I'm beginning to think there is something wrong with me. I can never get a job. It doesn't seem to matter what I go for: receptionist, cleaner, or shop assistant. Each time, I get declined.

"I can work any hours. I have no other commitments. I'm willing to start on a smaller salary, and I learn quickly." I fire off the same lines I always do.

Mr. Jordan places my resume in the center of his desk. "Have you held a receptionist position before?"

"I work for Alex Murphy, so taking calls is part of my job." Not the truth, but Sally will verify anything I say. I could claim to be the head chef, and she'd back me up.

"What else do you do for Mr. Murphy?"

"I'm his personal assistant. So errands, booking appointments, even getting his coffee." I smile at that, but I hate doing that particular job. The rest doesn't require me to be in his presence. With emails, my life has become somewhat easier, but bringing him his morning and evening coffee is a task I detest. Most times, he doesn't even notice me, but that's what's so messed up. I notice him. It sounds so stupid, but my soul recognizes him as the boy who brought me to life.

Then he dumped me without an explanation.

"Miss Greenwood?" Mr. Jordan speaks.

I curse myself. I zoned out again. "I do apologize. I'm a bit nervous." I rub my palms along my thighs like the action will make my lie believable. Like it might cover up the fact that my brain refuses to let Alex Murphy go.

"We will be in touch." Mr. Jordan's tone doesn't hold any enthusiasm. It's like words are just rolling off his tongue on autopilot.

He tugs at his silver tie as he looks at his screen. I'm dismissed.

"That's it?" I ask.

He glances at me and nods. "That's it, Miss Greenwood."

I messed up again.

"I'll do a trial run. Two weeks free of charge." I sound desperate. But I am. I need to get away from Alex Murphy. I refuse to live like this any longer. And lately, he wants me to join him at functions so I can be his slave and get his drinks and coffee.

I just can't anymore. The armor I wore to protect me is cracked and battered, and I need space from the Murphys. I need to start somewhere fresh. I can't exactly go far, or I'd have skipped the country. My mother's health keeps me here and in a job, as her medicines aren't cheap.

"I'll be in touch." Is that pity I see in his eyes?

"I didn't get the job?" I haven't left the chair. I'm drowning in dark waters, and I just feel like I'm seriously screwed.

"Miss Greenwood. I have other people to interview. We will be in touch."

I rise, and I want to tell him not to bother, that I already know the answer, but instead, I just need something more. "Why? Just please tell me. Am I not qualified enough? Did I come across as needy?"

The door behind me opens, and the man that led me here looks at Mr. Jordan, who holds up a hand. "Just a minute, Fredrick."

Fredrick leaves, and my heart races. Will someone finally answer me and explain what it is I'm lacking?

"Your resume is impressive. Working for the Murphys is impressive. Especially lasting over seven years. Your eagerness is also to be admired. You appear well dressed and professional, Miss Greenwood." He pauses.

"So…" I got the job? My heart triples in speed.

He opens his mouth to speak but closes it just as quickly. "So, we will be in touch." When he says the words, they sound like an afterthought. That's not what he was going to say. But I need to leave or else I'm sure I'll be escorted out by security.

***

The honks of horns and the smell of the city infiltrate my senses, but they don't disturb the overwhelming truth of defeat. Again and again.

I close my eyes and tilt my head back to breathe a lungful of air when a shoulder slams into me, nearly sending me to the ground. The guy with a brown briefcase mumbles a sorry but keeps walking. My phone buzzes in my jacket pocket, and I answer it as I start to walk.

"Boss is looking for you," Sally says.

I worm through the crowd before turning down an alleyway where I illegally parked my car. It hasn't been towed. I'm lucky like that. I never get tickets even though I break so many parking laws in the city.

"Do you know what he wants?" I ask as I get into my car. The sound of the city disappears. Rock music blares to life as I turn the ignition, cutting off Sally's response.

I quickly turn the volume down. "I didn't hear that, Sally. What did you say?"

"He didn't say what he wanted you for, but he only just sent down the request."

I glance at the clock in the dash of the car. "I'll be back in fifteen minutes. If he asks again, say I went to pick up his favorite coffee."

Sally snorts. "I would have used that excuse if he had asked."

I grin as I start to back out of the alleyway. "I'll see you soon."

I had ten bags of his favorite coffee beans in my trunk just in case he ever called me out on my lie. I disappeared sometimes once a week for interviews, and Sally was a gem, always covering for me, but at rare times like this, when he asked for me while I wasn't there, he never questioned my late appearance.

I arrive back at Alex's mansion, and my shoulders droop. If I could, I'd turn the car around and leave. The thought of never seeing Alex or his home again makes my stomach squirm.

I park my car with the rest of the staff. I won't have time to change, but it wouldn't matter if I entered Alex's office on stilts naked; he wouldn't notice me.

As I race through the back porch area, I nearly slam into Aidan, Alex's younger brother.

He reaches out and stops me from smacking into him. "What's the panic?" He smiles, but like all the Murphy brothers, their smiles never reach their eyes, yet Aidan is one of the kindest of them all. His brown eyes just seem softer than the rest. They aren't as hard as Alex's stare. I never clicked with Aidan like I did Alex, but we hung out sometimes when I was a kid. I mean, I practically lived in their home while I was growing up. My Mother was the staff manager, and she brought me to work with her. Instead of helping, I got to know the boys, and we had some great times.

"I took a long lunch break," I confess as Aidan releases me.

"You look very smart." He runs both his hands through his hair.

My cheeks heat, and I wrinkle my nose. "This old thing?" I say.

He grins. "You look like you could be coming from an interview."

My heart halts in my chest. I'm shaking my head. "Why would I do that? I already have a job." I'm babbling.

Aidan smiles again. "I'm just saying you look good, Nadia."

My cheeks burn. I'm such a fool. "Thank you."

Aidan departs, and I glance at the gold watch on my wrist. Shit. He's going to be pissed.

CHAPTER TWO

ALEX

Y OU LIVE BY THE sword; you die by the sword. These are words that have been ingrained into my brain. I lived by my father's standards, only I didn't die by them. He did. It was just by my hand.

I killed my father.

He had taken everything from me until there was nothing left. I'm empty, and I have no idea how to fix it.

A spark of light—that's how I see the handle of the door that pushes down. The light swells and pours into my office as Nadia, my PA, steps in. She avoids eye contact. In fact, I'd say she'd rather be anywhere but near me.

"Where were you?" I ask. I never question her. I know her every move. I know every interview she takes, every friend she makes, and every bit of food she buys. I know everything about her. There is nothing that I don't know about Nadia Greenwood. I know about every failed date because I made them that way.

"I had to go and get some more coffee beans, Mr. Murphy." She says each word with hate. Unlike the rest of my staff, Nadia doesn't hide her dislike for me.

I examine her from the tips of her black high heels, along her toned legs wrapped in a pencil skirt, and past her perfect-sized bust to her face. She doesn't look at me. No, Nadia could never do anything in half measures. She glares at me.

"You are doing the work of the caterers now?"

Green eyes fire up, and I'm sure if she were holding the beans, she'd throw them at me. I want her to act out. I want her to look alive. I want her.

I always have.

I refocus on my computer screen. "I have a meeting later that requires me to go out of town." I glance at her.

I will wipe the smile in her eyes right out. I tighten my hand around a pen. "You will accompany me."

Like sugar on a grease fire, her smile disappears. "I'm afraid that's not possible."

"Why is that, Miss Greenwood?"

"My mother needs me." There it is. The same excuse and the only one I will always allow. Does she know that? I'm sure Nadia does. She's smart. She sees beneath what people want her to see. She has a way of making me feel seen, and that's not always a good thing.

How much would she hate me if she knew I killed my father? That thought has me glancing back at the screen. My jaw tightens. She keeps refusing me at every turn, making everything impossible. I know she has a date this weekend with a Marcus Rodgers.

"You're such a good daughter." I can't keep the bitterness out of my words.

"I don't abandon people."

My throat catches at her words. She would never dare say such a thing to me. Is that what she thinks happened between her and me? Does she think I abandoned her?

She rubs her eyes, and I see the tiredness. "Is that all, Mr. Murphy?" Her voice is exhausted.

I want to see what's hiding behind that anger. I've killed people. I deal with the most dangerous men in Ireland, but Nadia, she fucking scares me. I nod, and before I can blink, she's gone.

I'm aware of the anger that circles around me like a vulture around a carcass. I'm staring at the door, wanting to go after her, wanting to demand that she lets me back in. When she left my world, she took every bit of goodness with her. She knew the power she wielded over me, and she used it to destroy me.

Then let her go, the voice whispers in my head. She's been trying to leave for a few years now, and even though the sight of her tortures me, I can't let her go.

I won't let her go.

Ever.

Even if this is our existence—my loving her with hate. Or her hating me from a place of love.

I run my hand along my face and try to banish my ruminating thoughts. I wasn't lying when I said I had to go out of town for a few days. All the main families of the Irish Mafia are meeting. Most of the talk will be about territory and politics. Having Nadia there would have made it almost bearable. I get up, and the heaviness of my conversation with my brother, Aidan, before Nadia arrived, weighs heavily on my shoulders. He is still looking ruthlessly for our father's killer.

The irony: Aidan had sat across from me, discussing tactics that allowed me to stay one step ahead.

Killing Rob, the ME, wasn't part of the equation. But I knew eventually, he would have to go. I took no pleasure in killing him. We had been friends, after all, and he had promised to keep my secret. It benefited his family in the sum of five million. That money no longer lies in his offshore account. I had my own accountant set it up so we could easily dismantle it with no paper trail.

I took no pleasure in planting a file in his office stating that Father was killed from blood loss.

Since William, our youngest brother, found our father hanging in his office and discovered that he couldn't have tied the knots, they'd deduced he was murdered. I knew I needed to do something.

It was such a minor detail, and yet it unraveled my whole setup.

Since they knew it wasn't a suicide, I used that once again to my advantage. While they looked for a blunt murder weapon, the real one lay in the bottom of my filing cabinet. A hunting knife that Father had given me for Christmas.

What's my end game in all of this? I have no idea. I've been trying to digest my emotions so that I can section them off, but it's not working. Sometimes it takes me a few days to understand what I'm feeling; other times, weeks. In this case, it appears months, and I still can't understand what I feel about my father's death.

It's a defect in my DNA. A defect that makes me seem emotionless. My first emotion is never my true one. Death makes me feel nothing. Zero. I have no reaction to it. It's after that things start to get interesting, and I know that emotion is my real one.

Like killing the ME. He begged and pleaded, but it was a means to an end. Putting a bullet in his head and dropping him in the river didn't cost me a second thought. Until now.

The demons of my mind are out for my blood, my remorse, and my guilt. As they chew me up, I revert my mind to something else.

This meeting with the Irish Mafia.

***

The plane touches down at Shannon Airport. I'm not the only private plane parked in the hangars. A limo is waiting for me, and Luke carries my bags to the trunk before returning to the driver's seat.

I reach for the coffee waiting for me in a heated holder. I missed my evening coffee that Nadia normally delivered to me. Not today.

I take a sip as Luke drives us to our destination.

The meeting is being held in a private house that caters to high-profile members for weddings and events; otherwise, its gates are closed to the public.

The entire building will be ours for the duration of our visit. As the limo rolls out of the hangar, my mind goes back to the conversation with Aidan. He leaned across my desk with a look of excitement in his eyes as he swore to me we were closing in on Father's killer.

I smiled a smile that he would never understand. A joke had wanted to spill from my lips. 'You're not closing in, Aidan. Why? Because you are sitting right in front of him.'

What would my brother do? He'd kill me. They all would. Even Jason, who isn't our brother but our cousin. He was raised in our household under the guise that he was, in fact, our brother.

I felt anger initially, but when the dust settled, I realized I hated him. He got out. Why couldn't it have been me who belonged to Frank and not Jason?

I was jealous of Jason's fucked-up past.

I glance out the window and try to stop my thoughts from eating me whole. The limo rolls up to the gates and stops. Luke talks, and we start to move again. I leave the coffee in the limo and climb out as the door is opened for me.

"Mr. Murphy." I'm greeted by a member of the staff—a butler who wears a top hat that reminds me of a conductor at a funeral. I get out, and Luke hands over my bags to the bellboy.

I climb the large stone steps up to the main doors, which are open. The warmth from the lights floods the space, and the noise consumes my senses. Each gaze lands on me, where they think I am the prey, but there isn't any competition here with all these predators. Thankfully, I'm one, too, and not prey.

I nod at Richard O'Reagan. It doesn't seem that long ago we had a meeting with the O'Reagans at Jack's wedding. A meeting that went very wrong. But, I won't forget how they gave nothing in return. I'm sure they already know that. I turn my attention to one of the O'Rourkes who control the West of Ireland. He's approaching me with a smug smile on his face. We are roughly the same age, in our late twenties. Some days I feel so much older.

"Alexander." The use of my full name seems strange.

I wrap my hand around his. "Reilan, how are you?"

"I'm good. Do you want to get a drink before this officially starts?" he asks, releasing my hand.

"Is this unofficial business?"

He grins. "You just look approachable."

I'd laugh at that. I know how I look. Most people get 'fuck off' vibes from me. "You look friendly, too." I return the false compliment.

He laughs and steps up beside me, so we walk together. "I never said you were friendly, Alexander. I just thought you would be the best to approach first with my idea."

A play on words. Fine.

We enter the bar and sit on leather chairs that hide us from prying eyes.

"So this idea of yours, what has it got to do with me?" I ask.

Reilan doesn't answer as a waiter swiftly places two glasses of brandy on the table and leaves. We had to fill in all our information before arriving so the service would be as seamless as possible. We are left alone, and I take a sip of the brandy.

"The Elders are going to make an offer today," Reilan starts.

Each district of Ireland is run by separate families. Four in total.

Reilan has ruled the West under a group of Elders, while the O'Reagans rule the East and have a foothold in the North. They have four kings who rule equally. As for the South, I solely control that. Our ways are different.

The North has one ruler, too, but it's still separated from the rest of the Irish. Bad blood that never thinned out. In fact, over time, even as the war died down, the undercurrent of hate grew thicker. Irish people never forgot what the English did.

"The offer is my sister. They want you to take her hand in marriage."

I don't react to that. Honestly, it doesn't surprise me. I alone control the south. Their having a stake in the South will make them more powerful. I'm expecting a lot of offers today, but not one of them will I agree to.

"When they make the offer, I'll think about it."

Reilan shifts closer, his face stern and serious. "I want you to say no."

He makes me curious, but I don't show my hand. I thought he would be pleading with me to say yes. "As I said, when the offer is given to me officially, I'll think about it."

I will say no, but he doesn't need to know that.

I'm ready to stand when he clamps his hand on my arm.

"Take your hand off me." He has no right to touch me.

He does. "Do you have sisters?"

"No," I answer dismissively.

"Okay, well, my sister doesn't want this. I mean, it's the twenty-first century. I don't want this for her either."

I glance around the room. Each corner is occupied with men in deep conversation. Making alliances.

"How noble," I say and get up.

Reilan rises too, and he's like a dog waiting for a bone. So I throw him one just to get rid of him. "I've already set my sights on someone who isn't your sister."

No, I've never had my sights on anyone except Nadia, and now I may have to act on all the fantasies I've had of making her mine.

I already know she won't make this easy.

But I refuse to take no for an answer.

CHAPTER THREE

NADIA

"Everything okay?" Eddie asks while dipping his head.

Running my hand along my forehead, I try to mop up some sweat. "Yeah, just another bad day at work." I don't want to talk about it, and I hope my tone implies as much.

But Eddie drops his hands and nods. "Do you want to talk about it?"

I do. I don't. I bend at the waist and pick up the dumbbells, hoping we can get on with my training session, but Eddie doesn't look like he's ready to get back to working out.

He's honestly been a rock for me the last year, and when I get lost in the pain of working out, I want to feel even more pain and push my body as hard as I can. If it gives me a few seconds from my thoughts, I'll do it. But lately, I can't seem to outrun my past. No matter how hard I run on the treadmill or how much weight I try to lift, it's always there.

Alex Murphy is ruining my life by just breathing air.

"I didn't get the job," I finally admit defeat and drop the dumbbells. Eddie doesn't say anything but passes me my bottle of water, which I gulp down. Not even an hour after leaving the interview, I got the email that said I didn't get the job, but they would keep my resume on file.

"Did they say why?" Eddie asks.

I shake my head and place the lid back onto the bottle.

"You know my offer still stands. I could do with a hand around here."

He's too good to me, but we both know that the gym isn't bringing in enough to support us both. I force a smile. "I know. But I'll find something."

"If you change your mind," Eddie offers as the door opens and another member arrives.

"Thanks, Eddie," I say as he pats me on the shoulder before going to log in the new arrival. I spend a few more minutes lifting weights before I decide I need to call it a day. I have to get home and check on my mother.

I shower and wave goodbye to Eddie on the way out. Opening the trunk to throw my gym bag in, I pause at all the packs of coffee beans for Alex. Jesus, he's everywhere. I drop my gym bag on the ground and gather all the coffee beans. With arms full, I walk to the dumpster at the side of the gym and toss in the beans. I have a moment of delight as I walk away. A small amount of regret seeps into my mind about dumping them. Maybe I was too hasty. But they have been rolling around in the trunk of my car for nearly two years. I'm not even sure if their freshness date has not passed.

I gather my gym bag off the ground and place it into the trunk, then close the lid before getting in and starting the car.

We live in a small, modest cottage on the outskirts of town. My mother loves her gardens, and I swear it's what keeps her alive. She worked most of her life for the Murphys, but one day changed everything for her. She collapsed at home one night, and when she was rushed to the hospital, they discovered a bubble in one of her lungs. Since then, her condition has worsened. Having half a lung removed was meant to help her, but it's more pressure on her one good lung. She spends most of her day wearing an oxygen mask. On good days, she manages to get out into the garden.

Home help is great, but they only cover a few hours in the middle of the day. Normally when I get home, they're gone.

I pull into the driveway, and when I enter the house, I find my mother in the armchair beside the window that's always left slightly open so she can smell all the scents of her garden. With a blanket across her knee and a fire smoldering, she stays warm.

She isn't wearing her mask, but the lines around her jaw are visible from hours of wearing it.

"Hello, sweetheart." She smiles at me as I lean down and place a kiss on her cheek.

"How was Sandra today?" I ask.

Sandra is her favorite home carer. The other one, Denise, drives her mad with too many questions.

"A dear, as always. Do you know she cleared out one of the kitchen cupboards for me? I honestly don't know what I would do without her."

Mother always kept a pristine home, and I often see how it itches at her to clean, but her body won't allow it. Her mind is still sharp, and even now, she tilts her head. "Everything alright? How was work?"

"Work was great. Alex sends his love," I lie easily. I could never tell her how much I want to get away from Alex. Because she would encourage me to do whatever I loved.

I sit down on the couch. A Scrabble board game is open on the coffee table, the remnants of her latest game left there.

"Did Sandra win again?" I ask.

"That was Denise who played, and I won." She smiles.

I chuckle, imagining the happiness that brought to my mother.

"She even accused me of cheating," Mam continues with a smile on her face.

"Some people don't like to lose. So what would you like for tea?" I need to get her food, and then I have a date that I actually don't want to go on. I already know it will fail. My dates either don't show or do and seem too bored with me that I never get a second date. I need to join one of those dating apps and see if I'm luckier, or I could adopt twenty cats and live here forever with my mother.

That thought has me off the couch.

"Just a light salad would be perfect, sweetheart. But there's no rush. I'm not overly hungry."

I love my mother dearly, but I always feel so caged within my life. Each turn I make leads me right back to where I started.

"I'll get it ready." I turn on the TV and leave my mother with the remote as she watches *The Chase*.

The small kitchen is warm from the lit stove. A radio plays away in the background, and I close my eyes, remembering what all the noises and smells felt like when I was a kid. Everything felt right in my home with my mother. She was full of life, always taking care of me. We were never apart. I loved the hours we played card games, watched TV, and spent the days at the Murphys' after school.

I had tried to teach Alex cards, but he always found a way to cheat. He didn't have to, but it was like he couldn't help himself. He had to figure out a way to game the system. Whether it would be to deal himself extra cards or keep some hidden, it didn't matter; Alex could never just be straight. I loved his boldness. At times, I would be so mad at him that he would laugh and apologize, telling me he wouldn't cheat again. Yet he always did.

I pause in slicing the tomatoes and lean heavily on the counter. How can anyone ever live up to him? Every man I meet, I compare to Alex Murphy.

I finish my mother's salad and take it to her in the sitting room. As she eats, I tidy up the Scrabble game and straighten the cushions. I pick up her slippers, then bring them over to her chair.

"I don't have to go," I say. I already don't want to go. Today has been such a bad day. Hopefully, tomorrow will be better.

"You are going. What's his name?" My mother's enthusiasm isn't infectious, but I muster as much happiness into my voice as I can.

"Marcus Rodgers," I say and try not to make eye contact.

"Oh, is he related to the Rodgers in the village?"

I shrug. "I'm not sure, Mother."

"You could ask him. Could be a good conversation booster." She nods at me.

"I'll file that away." I lean in and place a kiss on her forehead. "Right, I'll go get ready for my date with Marcus Rodgers, who may have relatives in the village."

Mother laughs softly, and I make my way to my small bedroom I've slept in my entire life. I really didn't think that at twenty-three I would still be here.

I opt for jeans and a red shirt. Not my finest clothes, but I'm not feeling like getting into a dress tonight.

My phone dings in my pocket, and I slide it out, smiling.

Sorry, I never got to say goodbye properly. Are you training again tomorrow? The message from Eddie is nice.

I'm not sure. I'll let you know in the morning if that's okay. I send the message back as I apply a small amount of makeup and tie my hair up into a high ponytail.

My mother is engrossed in one of her soaps. I don't go fully into the room. "I won't be late."

She waves a hand in my direction. "Don't you dare come home early. Go have fun, and you can tell me everything tomorrow."

The slight movement of the curtains has me stepping into the room. I reach to close the window.

"Leave it open," my mother says.

"Don't forget to close it." She often does, and the sitting room is often freezing in the mornings. I'm usually in here freezing as I chase daddy longlegs around the room, and I'm not a fan of the cold or creepy crawlers.

"I will."

I leave the house and drive into town. I park outside one of the local hotels, where I'm meeting Marcus. My stomach starts to squirm. Grabbing my bag and phone, I get out of the car and lock it as I make my way into the hotel lobby. It's nice and warm inside. Marcus agreed to meet me at the bar, so that's where I go. Only one other man is here; otherwise, the place is dead.

He isn't my date. I met Marcus through Eddie at the opening night of his newly located gym. A few words were exchanged, so I was surprised when he asked me out on a date.

I order a shandy. Half Budweiser, half 7up. I can have one drink and drive, but that's the driving limit. If the night goes well, I could always get a taxi home.

Time ticks away, and I keep checking my phone, waiting for Marcus to text. After two hours, I think it's a reasonable amount of time to text him and see where he is.

I order another drink. This time, I move to vodka and 7up. Several drinks later, and being the only one in the bar, I know he isn't coming.

I finish my drink and go to reception, where they call me a taxi. *Don't cry. Don't cry*, I chant as I wait outside in the dark for the taxi that rolls up. I get into the back and give him my address. I'll have to get another taxi in the morning to get my car. I arrange this with the driver as he drops me off at home. Walking up the sidewalk, I see the sitting room window is still open.

I curse my mother as I place the key into the door. I'll be hunting insects in the morning instead of nursing the hangover I'm sure I'll have from all the alcohol.

The house is pitch black. It takes me a moment to realize how odd that is. I pause and close the door slowly behind me. My mother always leaves the lamp on in the hall. I pass the sitting room door, and my heart seizes in my chest.

"Mother!" I'm on my knees. The alcohol evaporates as my panic soars. She's lying on the ground, not moving, and the fear chokes me as I check for a pulse.

Please don't be dead. Please don't leave me.

CHAPTER FOUR

ALEX

T HE ROOM IS PULSATING with the most powerful people in Ireland. Some of them even have power that extends abroad. Tables have been lined across from one another, and the seats are slowly filling up. Jason would have accompanied me if I had asked him. I don't like asking people for anything. I sit down on the right side of the room, where no one else has sat.

Across from me are the four kings of the East. Jack and Richard O'Reagan are deep in conversation. Cillian slides in beside them with a sullen expression. Shay juts out his chin at me in greeting. I nod a greeting back, and he smirks while sitting down. He hasn't taken his gaze off me. He's one of the kings I trust the least. He slips a packet of cigarettes out of his pocket. This is a nonsmoking hotel; signs have been posted everywhere, but I don't think anyone would dare tell Shay O'Reagan not to light up here.

"Alexander." Dillon O'Rourke sits to my left. His graying hair and small black glasses make him appear like a normal person. He doesn't hold the air most Mafia leaders do. He's one of the Elders of the West and holds an enormous amount of power. My father always made time for him.

"Dillon, how are you?" I ask.

He unbuttons his navy suit jacket and crosses his hands in front of him on the table. The gesture is almost open and nonthreatening. But I know he has selected the seat beside me to talk about his daughter.

"I've had better days," Dillon says with a smile. It's then you see the gangster in him as he flashes me a mouth full of gold teeth. It's an odd contrast on the old man's face. "Being here isn't something I look forward to, but it comes with the territory."

I'm aware of Shay still watching me, but my focus is taken up by Reilan, who sits beside his father. He's sporting a navy suit, also. Unlike the rest of us, who seem to be dressed in black. Even Shay is wearing a suit. Not even for a funeral would he get dressed up.

"Alexander," Reilan greets me with a fake look of surprise, as if we didn't share a drink and a chat about his sister.

"Reilan," I greet back. I agree with Dillion; this is the last place I want to be. But it's twice a year that all the Mafia leaders of Ireland meet. The room fills up with more Elders from the West. I try to focus on Dillon's words about smaller gangs breaking across the border from the North and trying to control the drug trade that isn't theirs to control. Young and upcoming greedy thugs is what he calls them.

"Dad, leave it out." Reilan sounds exasperated, and I can only imagine how much he must have to listen to. When the final seats are filled, the doors are closed by two security men, and I'm grateful for it so I don't have to keep meeting Shay's grinning face. He's starting to piss me right off.

"Thank you all for coming." Mark O'Rourke, Reilan's uncle, takes center stage. The walls around us are lined with security. Each person with their own security team and also the security that's part of the hotel. These would be the highest-ranking security to be placed in this room and be privy to our operations. Death is the penalty for speaking about what takes place in this room. In my time, I've never heard of that level of betrayal.

On the one hand, with the sheer amount of security, we were in the safest place, but I didn't fear the people outside these walls. On the other hand, the people inside were far more dangerous.

"The first matter is the attacks on shipments near the east-south docks, where I know a lot of trade comes through. A young gang seems to be responsible. We haven't managed to stop them yet, but with joint forces, we should be able to combat this."

"We have men watching the area and have put out word of a shipment coming in. We will be there to catch them." Richard O'Reagan speaks up. His voice carries across the room. My gaze is once again drawn to Shay, who is no longer watching me. He's engrossed in the black device on the desk in front of him.

"We will send some of our men to assist." Mark waves his hand in the O'Reagan's general direction. It's Jack who bristles. His spine is rod straight. From the tightness of his jaw, it's obvious he wants to interject and decline the offer. But that would be seen as an insult. Richard nods his approval, but he doesn't appear any happier than his brother.

"We will also send some of our men," I say, knowing I don't want the O'Reagans and O'Rourkes handling anything without my knowledge. The flow of shipments coming into Ireland affects us all, as the docks are the most secure. Nearly everyone is bought off, and it's neutral ground for the Irish Mafia. An agreement that's been in place for a long time. The only people we don't share the docks with are the North. If they were allowed to step into our territory, I'm sure the O'Hanlons would try to stake a claim on the land, and frankly, they have taken enough from us already, but that's history tied up in politics.

Mark sits down, and Jack is the one who gets up and walks to the front of the room. Out of all the O'Reagans, he's the one I like the most. He's an honest criminal, if there even is such a thing, and I would consider his word as truth. Unlike his cousin Shay, whom I wouldn't trust as far as I could throw him, and with his bulk, that wouldn't be far.

Jack lays out his plan, and we all agree to have our men at his disposal so we can put an end to the disruption. Some young and upcoming thugs will always be a threat, but if we show unity and power and squash it instantly, it sends a message to others: to think before they act. Lately, that's becoming harder with how brazen the youth are.

The conversation moves to the Russians, who have taken up residency in Ireland. They control small areas, not enough to really affect us. I get sideway glances because my brother Jason is now a negotiator for the Russians, a deal he took to save his skin when he killed their negotiator, who hadn't deserved to live because he had abused his sister, who is now Jason's wife.

"On other matters, I want to propose an arranged marriage." Dillon goes up front once Jack sits back down. I'm ready for all the focus to turn on me.

"My daughter has come of age, and she's ready to do her part for the family."

I don't have to look at Reilan to know he's watching me. I focus on Dillon, who's speaking directly to me. "I think a partnership would be wise."

I nod. "I'm sure your daughter will make a great wife. I'll consider it," I state plainly.

Dillon smiles before using his index finger and pushing his glasses back up his nose. "Don't wait long. We do have others interested."

I give a nod and a forced smile like I will consider it. After more politics, the meeting comes to an end, and security files out along with their leaders. I'm left with the hotel security, whom I dismiss and retire to my room. One more day and I can leave. Tomorrow is more relaxed, as we have the opportunity to make alliances or seek information that might help. For me, it's the day I hate most. I won't ask any of them for anything. And I won't grant any of them anything, either.

Each of us are staying on different floors, which will allow me to sleep easier. The queen-size bed is lost in the large suite that has a seating area and a bar. The bathroom can be seen through the glass walls. Not my kind of décor, but I won't complain.

I remove my tie and leave it on the bed. Checking my phone, I see I have a missed call from Aidan and one from Edmond, one of my men. I'm in no mood to call either back.

My thoughts take me to the bar, where I pour out half a glass of vodka. Knocking it back, I allow the substance to burn slowly down my throat before I give my final swallow. Closing my eyes, I summon the image of my father standing in front of me, arguing, but the memory dissolves at the soft knock on my room door. I walk over as a note is slid under the door, then pick it up, not bothering to open the door. I'm fairly certain I already know who the note is from as I open it to read the words scrawled inside.

Remember what we talked about.

There is no signature, but I don't need one. It's Reilan, as he's the only person I've talked to privately. Tomorrow, I'm sure he will find me and plague me. His love for his sister is to be admired, but his naïve approach is not. He will become an Elder, and I'm not sure he'll be someone I would align myself with. He carries a weakness in his love for his sister. If I didn't already want Nadia, I would take his sister, not out of spite, but as a lesson to show him my power. Make it easy to manipulate him when he steps into his elder role. My father would have my head for turning this opportunity down, but he's not here.

I strip off my clothes and leave them on the bench at the foot of the bed. The heavy gold silken duvet will surely make sleeping hard, as my duvet covers are cotton. But once I lie down, I fall into a dreamless sleep. I never dream, but my sleep is light, and the smallest of noises wake me. Even the soft buzzing of my vibrating phone on the bedside table.

Aidan's name flashes up on the screen again. It's three in the morning. This must be important.

"Is something wrong?" I answer, sitting on the edge of the bed.

"I thought you would be asleep." Aidan sounds alert.

"I was. But I'm awake now."

"Edmond has been trying to ring you."

"Has something happened?" I snap, rising to my feet.

"It's nothing major, but he was insistent that I call you, insistent enough to call me all evening. There was a break-in at Nadia's house."

"Is she dead?"

"Don't sound so hopeful." Is that spite I hear in Aidan's voice? "No, she's at the hospital with her mother. She wasn't there when the attack happened."

"Thanks for letting me know." I pick up my shirt and slide my arm into the sleeve.

"Now I can finally go back to sleep, and so can you." Aidan yawns.

"I'll call you tomorrow." I end the call and finish getting dressed. I grab my few belongings and leave the hotel room. Security is alert and stationed close to the large gold elevator doors. One of them reaches across and presses the button. The doors spring open, and I step inside. I'm waiting for the fear and panic, but right now, I feel nothing. I just know I need to get to her.

Edmond answers on the first ring. "What happened?"

"There was a shift change. Jake was second, and when he arrived, Duggy was already gone. So it happened before Jake got there. Nothing was taken, but the mother was attacked."

"Where is Nadia now?" I ask as my brain calculates the situation with ease. Someone must have been watching the house. If they took nothing, then it wasn't a burglary. Did Duggy have something to do with it? Did he turn a blind eye? Straight away, I don't think that's it. Duggy is loyal. But loyalty can break easily in our line of work.

"She's at the hospital with her mother. I'm here now," Edmond says.

The elevator doors open, and I step out into the foyer.

"And Duggy?" I ask as I stop by the desk and return my keycard.

"You are leaving, Mr. Murphy?" the receptionist asks.

I cover the phone. "A family emergency. Could I have a pen and paper?" I ask, and she hands me a pad of hotel stationery. I tear off a piece of paper.

"Duggy is with Jake. He swears he left for his daughter's birthday. He feels terrible."

"Tell Jake to stay with him until I get back," I inform Edmond before hanging up.

I leave a note for Dillon O'Rourke explaining I left due to a family situation. As I depart the hotel, all I can think of is getting to Nadia and seeing with my own eyes that she's safe.

CHAPTER FIVE

NADIA

MY MOTHER'S HANDS ARE wrinkled and coated in age spots. I hadn't noticed them before, but I've been staring at her limp hand in mine for hours. A tube runs from her hand up to the IV bag that's pumping medication for pain relief into her already damaged body.

My thumb runs along her skin, and it gathers and shifts with the movements. My gaze travels to her face. An oxygen mask covers most of her lower jaw. She's so pale. Old. How had I not noticed how old she had become? Her illness has taken a toll on her body. Her kidneys aren't working like they used to. I hadn't known that her condition had started to affect other organs. God, she has kept so much from me. If she hadn't been hurt and brought to a hospital, I don't think I'd ever have known just how much she had deteriorated in such a short amount of time.

Two emotions clash and battle for dominance. I'm angry that she kept me in the dark but sad that she felt the need to keep this truth hidden from me. Her body was failing, and there was nothing they could do. Major surgery wasn't something the doctor wanted to perform, not with her weakening body, but the end result would be kidney failure; that's assuming her lung didn't collapse again.

The air in the room feels thin, and I release my mother's hand, placing it with care on the white hospital sheets. She hasn't woken since being brought in, but her injuries are minimal from the attack; it's her ongoing condition that had her admitted.

I run my hands across my face like I can banish the image of her lying on the sitting room floor. For a moment, I thought she was dead. The fear was all-consuming. A fear that I hadn't felt in a long time. My hands tremble as I attempt to get a cup of water from the cooler. The plastic cup crinkles, and the noise seems loud against the silence of the room. The only other sound demanding my attention is the beeping of the machine. I pull the red blouse away from my chest to allow some cool air to filter onto my flushed skin.

I loosen my grip on the cup and fill it with water. As I walk to sit back down at my mother's bedside, I spot a man through the small window in the door. He's leaning against the wall across from my mother's room. Our eyes meet, and he looks familiar, but I can't place from where.

As I continue to stare at him, my fingers grip the cup. What if he's the man who attacked my mother? Is he here to finish the job? Cold water spills across my hand, and I dance back from the splash as I break eye contact with the man. When I look back up, he's gone. My mind races to memorize his face, the uneven skin that would suggest childhood acne, and the deep brown eyes, along with the gold earring and the brown leather jacket.

Everything disappears as a figure blocks my view, and the door opens.

My heart thumps heavily in my chest, and if the cup hadn't been nearly empty, I'm sure I'd be soaked.

"Alex?" What the hell is he doing here? His gaze takes me in from the crown of my head all the way to the water at my feet. His dark eyes give nothing away, and when he steps in and closes the door behind him, my confusion grows. "What are you doing here?"

He walks past me and gathers some blue paper towels from a dispenser on the wall before returning to me.

"You didn't turn up to work," he says simply before he bends down and cleans the water at my feet.

"What?"

He rises, his fist tightening around the wet paper. "How is your mother?" he asks, but he hasn't taken his eyes off me.

I take a peek at my watch. It's ten in the morning. God, where did the night go? "I'm an hour late," I mumble. "Do you stalk all your employees?" I glare at him, pissed and still feeling confused. "Aren't you supposed to be out of town?" I fire as my suspicion deepens.

He walks away to the trash bin and steps on the pedal. The lid opens, and he deposits the wet tissue inside. "Let me take you home."

He's so calm. He always is.

I place the plastic cup onto my mother's table at the end of her bed. "I'm not going home. And why won't you answer my questions? Why are you here?"

He turns to me, and my stomach flips.

"You never turned up to work," he states like I'm overreacting.

I want to argue and fight, but my mother groans, and all is forgotten. I pick up her hand. "I'm here, Mam. I'm right here," I tell her. Tears burn my throat and nose with relief, with fear of what she will say when she opens her eyes.

"Nadia." She blinks a few times before focusing on my face.

I keep the tears at bay. "I'm here," I repeat.

Her focus shifts to Alex, who's standing behind me. I can feel the heat roll off his body. I want him to leave. This situation is emotional enough without me having to deal with how he makes me feel.

"Alexander. How are you?" My mother asks politely.

"I'm good, Miss Greenwood. But how you are is more important." When Alex speaks, he sounds so impartial. I have no idea if he really is concerned. I want to glance at him, but I keep focusing on my mother.

"Sore." She reaches up as if to touch the back of her head where the burglar struck her, but her stiff body has her hand falling back onto the bed. Sadness fills her gaze.

"It's okay, Mam. You're safe now." I smile, but it doesn't take the worry away from her eyes.

"Did you see who did this?" Alex asks.

I look at him, but he's focused on my mother. "You can leave that to the Gardaí," I bite. Where did he get off arriving here? Because I'm late for work, and now questioning my mother, who just woke up?

I get his attention and instantly don't want it, but he won't harass my mother.

"I didn't. It was so quick and sudden," my mother answers him, though she shouldn't, and she takes off the mask, oxygen seeping out.

"Why don't you leave," I suggest, releasing my mother's hand and turning to face Alex, who's standing too close. I'm expecting him to step away, but he doesn't.

"I'll take you home." He says it this time like that's what's going to happen. I'm ready to protest when my mother speaks.

"Go home, Nadia. Rest. You look exhausted."

I'm back at my mother's bedside. "I'm not leaving you."

She gives me a soft smile. "I'm just going to sleep for a while." This time, she takes my hand, but she looks up at Alex.

"I don't want her left alone."

My body goes rigid. "Mam, I can take care of myself," I object.

"I won't. You have my word," Alex answers as if I haven't spoken, and I watch as my mother nods, and a look of relief passes her face before she sinks into the pillows.

"Let me rest, and get some sleep yourself." My mother delivers her words like she's fit and healthy and in control of the situation. I can't move.

She squeezes my hand. "Please, Nadia. Let Alex take you home."

I want to argue, but I won't upset her. I nod. He can take me home, but he isn't coming inside.

"I'll call the nurse once I'm home. I'll be back in a few short hours."

"Don't rush. I need my rest." She closes her eyes, and I release her hand. I want to confront her about her health, but I know this isn't the time.

I turn around, and Alex takes a few steps away from me. But I pause, and he waits by the door. When I gather my bag and move toward him, he opens the door for me. Out in the hallway, I look for the man with brown eyes and a gold earring, but I don't see him.

Alex doesn't ask me any questions, and his silence is heavy. The air outside is cool, and the breeze slips through my red silk blouse. I wrap my hands over my arms to fight off the cold as I follow Alex to his Jaguar. He opens the passenger door for me, and without thanking him, I slip inside and pull on my seat belt.

The moment he's in the car, the space feels suffocating. I'd open a window if I wasn't so cold. Alex starts the car and turns on the heat.

As we drive, my chest tightens. At first, I think it's from being around Alex, but I soon realize the closer we get to home, the idea of going inside is terrifying. What if the man comes back? The house won't feel the same. Someone broke in and hurt my mother. Was he an addict looking for money? I have no idea what was stolen. We don't have much.

"I have to go to the Gardaí station and make a statement," I say out loud as I play through the night like it was a lifetime ago.

After I found my mother, I dialed 999. The Gardaí got there in ten minutes, along with an ambulance, while I kept my fingers on my mother's neck, trying to remind myself that she was alive. All the while, the fear of whoever attacked her returning kept me looking over my shoulder. I hadn't felt that kind of fear before. I couldn't leave my mother, yet I was so vulnerable.

My throat burns again, and as Alex pulls up outside the house and turns off the car, I don't move. He doesn't ask questions as he unbuckles his belt and climbs out. The cold breeze gets in for a moment, but as he closes his door, I'm back in a warm silent cocoon.

I watch Alex as he strides around the car and opens my door, allowing a blast of wind in. It wakes me up, and I get out. He closes the door as I make my way to the house that seems almost foreign. Digging my hand into my pockets to get the keys should be a simple task, but I have to apologize as I struggle.

Alex doesn't speak but clears his throat. Once I have the keys out, I glance at him. Why is he still standing here?

"I don't know if I'll be back to work tomorrow," I say.

Isn't that why he's here? To make sure I return to work. I'm not even a good worker. If anything, I don't know how I've lasted so long at the job.

"That's fine," he answers. I hate his monotone.

"You can leave now," I bite out. Whose boss checks up on them like this? I place the key in the door and pause. I don't want to go inside.

I turn to ask Alex why he's still standing there when he slides his arm between me and the door, pushing me to the side as he turns the knob and opens the door. He leaves me standing on the porch as he walks inside.

"What are you doing?" I ask.

He doesn't answer as he disappears into the sitting room. The cold drives me inside, and I close the front door. Alex reappears and walks down the hall.

"What are you doing?" I ask again as he disappears into the kitchen. I follow him. By the time I reach the kitchen door, he's already stepping back into the main hall and down the small one that leads to the bedrooms and bathroom.

"I'm making sure it's safe," he says as he opens the bathroom door. The next room is mine and I've had enough. Ducking under his arm, I press my back against the door, stopping him from entering.

"That's enough," I say firmly.

"I need to check inside the room, Nadia." Alex saying my name transforms his voice. It's like someone breathed life back into the dead. He's so close I can smell his cologne.

"This is my bedroom." All of a sudden, I'm aware of our small home and how it differs from his mansion.

"All the more reason to check," he states and shifts while reaching for the door handle.

I slide closer, stopping him. "I don't think anyone is waiting inside my bedroom."

"That's where I would wait." His words are low, and his gaze dips to my mouth.

My body roars to life, and I have an overwhelming feeling to push him away. My mind screams that I can't do this again. I can't see him as Alexander; it's already cost me too much. I can't see him as the boy I loved. He's my boss. But the idea of Alex waiting in my room like a predator has me looking away and stepping aside. I fold my arms over my chest as he enters my bedroom. Without looking into the room, I'm imagining what he sees. A single bed, a chest of drawers. Tidy, devoid of life.

He caused that.

My nails dig into my palms as I wait for him to leave my room, but he's still inside. I have a split-second wondering if someone is inside. I spin around. He's standing close to the bed, just looking around. His shoulders are tense, but as I scan the room, I don't see anything, only my simple room.

Yet, why is he still in my room? He walks to my chest of drawers, and I want him out of my room. This all feels inappropriate for a boss/employee relationship.

His hand reaches out to touch a jewelry box my mother gave to me; it was her mother's. Then I snap. I can't have him taint any more of me.

"Get out of my room." My words are loud and edged with panic.

His gaze snaps to me, and I grit my teeth.

We stare at each other for what feels like an eternity before he takes one final look at my room and departs. He doesn't go into my mother's bedroom but glances in from the open doorway. Yet, my space now reeks of Alex Murphy. Just great.

"Are you satisfied?" I ask as he steps back into the hall.

He closes my mother's bedroom door. "Not yet," he replies bluntly.

"Do you want to check the attic?" I've had enough.

He pauses like that's an option. I exhale. "It was a burglary. It's over now. I've never heard of a burglar hanging around." As I say the words, I think I'm trying to convince myself that when Alex leaves and I'm alone, I will be safe.

But I don't think I'll ever be safe again. As Alex watches me, I realize how rude I'm being. I must sound so ungrateful, regardless of his intentions. He brought me home and checked the house.

"Thank you for bringing me home, but I'm fine now, and I'll call when I'm coming back to work." I can't miss much time; with my mother in the hospital, the bill will run up daily.

Alex gives me a once-over. "Let me make you something to eat."

I'm left with my mouth hanging open as he walks past me and into my kitchen like this is alright.

It's not.

Not even close.

CHAPTER SIX

ALEX

S HE'S SEETHING. SHE'S READY to explode. She wants me gone. I want to smile. I've never seen her so alive. I don't want this moment to change. I want it to stay the same.

"You're not making me food." Her small delicate fingers curl into fists.

"Didn't you tell your mother you would ring the nurse once you got home?" It's a low blow to distract her.

She mumbles softly under her breath and rummages through her bag. When she extracts her cell, she glares at me before turning away. While she's occupied on the phone, I slip into the kitchen. The kitchen is small and tidy, but what I notice more is the feeling of warmth and comfort that fills the tiny space. I think I may like it here.

I unbutton my suit jacket as I take in the egg-blue cupboards; I wonder if Nadia picked the color. Removing my jacket, I place it onto the back of one kitchen chair. The small wooden table holds only two chairs.

I open the fridge and remove mushrooms, eggs, cheese, ham, and scallions. Placing everything onto the counter, I pause as Nadia's voice grows closer but moves away again.

I roll up my sleeves before placing the skillet on the stove, then add a dash of oil before turning on the burner. As I cut the mushrooms, I think of her room. It was stuck in a time warp; that's what it felt like to me, like the room hadn't caught up with the woman.

"This isn't necessary." Nadia's voice is low from the kitchen doorway.

I ignore her comment and place the mushrooms in the hot skillet. They sizzle slightly. "How is your mother?" I ask. I can imagine her grinding her teeth, and this time, I glance at her. I don't want to miss watching her emotions play out across her features.

Her hand tightens around her phone. "The nurse said she was asleep." Nadia places the phone onto the counter and steps into the kitchen. "Who cleaned up the sitting room?"

I return to chopping the rest of the ingredients. "One of my men," I answer as I add everything to the pan and give it a mix. I open several cupboard doors, looking for a mixing bowl for the eggs.

"What are you looking for?" Annoyance fills Nadia's voice as she appears at my elbow.

"A mixing bowl."

She bends at the waist and takes out a cream mixing bowl. She won't meet my eye as she hands it to me.

"Thank you for having someone clean it up." She sounds so begrudging.

"You can thank Edmond when you see him." He had organized the cleanup.

Her gaze darts up to my face. "Alex." Her brows knit closer together. She's going to tell me to leave again. I won't, but instead of allowing her the opportunity, I reach across her and pick up two eggs and crack them in the bowl before adding two more. Nadia gives up and drifts away to the table as I whisk the eggs and add them to the pan.

She's observing me with a look I can't decipher. "Could you make the coffee?"

Her brows pinch in a look of pain, but instead of fighting me, she puts on the kettle. I flip the omelet and get two plates. Cutting the portion in two, I give Nadia the large piece.

By the time I place the plates and cutlery onto the table, Nadia has returned with two cups of coffee. I accept mine and sit. Nadia doesn't. She's staring down at the tiny table with the two steaming heaps of food.

I start eating mine. She finally sits down, her perfume dancing around me, and I inhale before looking at her. She's awkward eating her food. In time, she will learn to relax. My phone vibrates in my trousers pocket, and I ignore it. I manage to eat a few more bites before the buzzing starts again. Nadia can hear the noise in the silence of the room.

"Will you please answer that?" Her abrupt words and angry eyes have me getting up and fishing the phone from my pocket. I'm tempted to power it off, but I answer Aidan as I leave the kitchen and make my way outside.

"How was the meeting?" he asks.

Two of my men are stationed at the small set of white gates that lead to Nadia's house. They have always stayed out of sight, but that can't happen anymore. I was lucky tonight that she wasn't here. That she didn't get hurt. A wave of anger has me tightening my hand on the phone.

"It went fine. We must send some of our men over to the docks for the O'Reagans. I'll give you all the information later."

"Okay," Aidan responds, and I wait. He didn't ring me to ask about the meeting.

"I found the solicitor, and I'm going to give him a surprise visit. Do you want to come?" I look back up at the white bungalow. Everything about Nadia's home is simple, yet functioning. I envy her simple life at times.

"No. I'm tied up with something at the minute," I say. "But do keep me informed of your findings." It doesn't matter what the solicitor has to say. Everything is above board. My father had signed over fifty percent of the business to Frank. It wasn't a ploy on Frank's behalf but the stupidity of my father's borrowings, and in the end, the only way to pay Frank was with such an enormous stake in the business.

I enter the house and walk down the hall. Once I reach the kitchen doorway, I pause. Nadia isn't sitting; she has barely eaten any food. Instead, she leans against the kitchen counter. She wears a look of steel. She's chewed over whatever she's about to say since I left.

I don't rush into the kitchen but allow myself to really see Nadia. Would this be what it feels like to come home from work and find Nadia waiting for me in the kitchen?

"I want you to leave," she finally says.

I nod. "You might want me to leave, but I can't do that."

She shakes her head and pushes away from the counter. "Why not?" Her voice cracks with unfallen tears.

Her question awakens so much inside me. I've been numb since I received the news about the attack on her mother, and all of a sudden, I get a rush of protectiveness, a rush of anger, a rush of lost time if she had been hurt.

"Do you think this was a regular burglary?" I question, taking a step toward her. "This was planned. You were a target." I tighten my jaw when I allow those words to sink in. As Nadia takes them in, fear drains the color from her face. That wasn't my intention.

"A target?" she repeats. She folds her arms across her chest.

"Because you work for me. So, it's my responsibility now to keep you safe."

She drops her arms to her side. "Keep me safe. You think whoever did this is coming back?"

The last thing I want is to scare her. But Nadia isn't fragile like other women. "I don't know."

Silence follows, and I wait for Nadia to speak. She's going to give in and let me stay; her blue eyes soften, and I feel a sense of victory that makes me want to smile.

"I'm not your responsibility, Alex. I'm your employee."

I read that wrong. She wasn't giving in after all. A smile dances on my lips, but I don't let it fully form. That would surely piss her off. But I shouldn't have thought she would give in that easily. "As my employee, you are my responsibility." If this were any other employee, I wouldn't be standing in the kitchen feeding them; she has got to know that.

"If your family thought so much about responsibility, then why didn't your father think it was his responsibility to help my mother? Why just let her fend for herself when she gave all her life to serve your family?" Her anger goes to new heights, and I've taken a step toward her.

My father took care of her mother. He cleared her mortgage. She still receives a weekly salary. I'm close to retaliating, but I pause. Why didn't her mother tell her this?

"I'm not my father." That much is true. I keep moving until her back is against the kitchen counter. "You can keep fighting me, Nadia, but I am going to keep you safe." My gaze drops to her bow-shaped lips. A kiss. The thought seems so far away from reality.

"I don't need you to keep me safe." Her anger fuels her words. She's being overly difficult. I understand she doesn't like me, but I didn't think her dislike sank this low. I want to ask her why she's so angry, but something I have learned about Nadia is: show her weakness, and she will use it. There's only one way of doing this.

"Pack a bag. We're leaving." I'm still staring at her lips, and I finally look away and take a step back. She's ready to combust.

"*You* are leaving."

I walk out of the kitchen and enter the small sitting room, where her mother was attacked. Some bastard thought it was okay to trample on my territory and hurt what's mine. I pick up the remote and turn on the TV. I sink into an armchair, and when Nadia storms into the room, I try to appear relaxed as I watch TV.

"What are you doing?"

"If you won't come with me, I'll have to stay here."

She's ready to speak when my phone starts buzzing again. I glance at the screen—Dillon O'Rourke. He isn't ringing to see about my family emergency. I'm sure he's ringing for an answer about his daughter.

"This is ridiculous." Nadia sounds exasperated. I'm a patient man, but I'm starting to feel my control slip.

She's glaring down at me, and no matter how angry she is, I can't leave her alone. Yet, I can't stay. The only way I can protect her is at my home.

She's not going to give in, and I didn't want it to come to this, but she has left me no choice. Calmly, I pick up the remote and turn off the TV, plunging us into a brief silence. I'm about to tell her to pack a bag, but the defiance in her stance has me getting up instead. She follows me into the kitchen, where I roll down my sleeves and put on my suit jacket.

"If anything happens, I'll call." She thinks I'm leaving.

I turn and raise both brows at her.

She swallows. "I promise."

"Hmm" is all I say as I walk past Nadia, down the small hall, and into her room. I open the top drawer of her dresser. Neatly folded tops land on the bed.

"Alex, you can't do this."

I ignore her and pull open the second drawer. It's her trousers. I take out a few pairs, and they join the tops on the bed. I glance around the room and spot a suitcase on top of the wardrobe. I take it down and start to unzip it.

"You're overreacting."

Pushing her clothes inside, I glance at her. "I have two men stationed outside your house."

She opens her mouth, but I turn to her to make myself clear. "There have always been men stationed outside your house. This attack was planned, Nadia."

Fear swims in her eyes, and I think I'm finally getting through to her.

I reach the dresser when her small hand lands on my sleeve. The contact is minimal, but it may as well be five hundred men holding me back.

"I'll pack the rest." Her small voice has me following her hand up to her face.

I nod, unable to speak with her closeness. She has always gotten so deeply under my skin, but now she's in my bloodstream, and I can't stop it.

I don't want to.

"Don't take long," I issue and step away from her. I need air.

CHAPTER SEVEN

NADIA

MY MIND IS RACING with so many questions. Like how long have his men been watching me? Why would he place men outside my home? Have I always been a target? Why? For being a staff member? Does everyone have security? They must. God, I didn't realize we would ever be targets.

My body is going through an onslaught of emotions being around Alex, thinking of my mother and the idea that some strange man was in my home. I finish packing the suitcase. When I leave my bedroom, Alex is standing in the hallway. His stature is always so composed, but I've seen snippets of a man under the stiff façade. Seeing behind his indifference and monotone is frightening because feelings come crashing back with an intensity that's hard to bear right now. My fingers grip the handle of the suitcase, and I hesitate.

Alex tilts his head like he's getting ready to jump into the ring for round five hundred.

"This will just be for a few nights, until things cool down," I say.

He nods instantly. I don't trust that. When he takes the suitcase from my hand, I grab my handbag from the kitchen. He cleaned up while I was packing. Domesticated Alex is doing funny things to my heart.

Closing the front door, I feel a sense of relief leaving the house. But I pause the moment I see Alex speaking to two men close to the gate. Their words are brief, and they depart as he walks back to the car. I watch them leave as he opens the car door for me.

"Who was that?" I ask.

"My security."

God, hearing there were men watching the house was one thing, but seeing them outside makes this all more real. I get into the car and wait until Alex starts the car.

"Does every staff member have security outside their home?"

Alex reverses out of the driveway. "No."

I want to ask why us. But maybe his father did take care of my mother—maybe not financially but by leaving men stationed outside the house. I don't ask any more questions. My mother was the longest-working staff member, that's why, and she would have been the only one who served under Alex's father. Everyone else started with Alex and not his father. That's the conclusion I have come to.

The drive to Alex's isn't far, and I wish I had my car. "I need to pick my car up." I stare out the window at all the passing trees.

"Where is it?" Alex asks in his usual monotone.

"At the Newgrange Hotel." I peek at him, and his gaze bounces from me to the road. The heat in the car and the smell of his cologne make me roll down the window.

His eyes ask the question that his lips don't voice, but it's none of his business why my car is there.

"I'll have someone pick it up."

I want to object, but I give in to this one small thing. We arrive at the house, and once the car stops, I don't wait for Alex to open my door. Being here has me back in work mode. When I reach the trunk of the car, Alex is already there taking out my luggage. My God, what will everyone else say?

What will Sally say? Is Sally safe? Would someone attack her? I have so many questions. Alex leads me into his home. I'm so used to arriving through the back door that it feels strange, and the space looks different. The knots in the wooden floor always bothered me. Seeing them from this angle don't make them any better. The knots appear every three paces; I don't like how unnatural it appears. I can't explain it.

Alex carries my suitcase toward the large stairs; the wrought iron balusters and their intricate design have always had my respect—well, the creator does. Some of the features in Alex's home are stunning. At times, I've been grateful to have seen such grandeur. I won't ever live this life, but I get to see someone else who does up close.

My shoulders tighten as I climb the stairs, and my hand runs along the polished wood of the banister. Celine, one of the cleaners, dips her head in greeting to Alex and moves past. Her gaze grows a little wider when she sees me. I smile, but she doesn't return the sentiment.

It's not malice that has most of the house staff turning away from me; they know I've been here since a child, so they see me as part of the house or the Murphys.

I'm staring at Alex's wide shoulders, and my stomach fizzles like a lid being taken off a shaken can of soda. He slows down at his room, and the fizz climbs up my throat, but he continues to walk and stops at what I know to be a guest room. Alex opens the double doors and places my bag onto the floor. As I enter, my phone dings.

I search for the device. When I take it out, I realize it's a message and not a call from my mother. I open the message from Eddie.

Will I see you this evening? You must tell me about the date.

Eddie makes me feel normal for almost a second, and I release a breath as I stare at his words. When I look up, Alex is watching me.

"Since I'm staying here, I'll be back to work tomorrow." I duck my phone behind my back; his gaze tracks my movements.

"No. Rest and go see your mother. I'll let you get settled," Alex says like I'm going to unpack. That won't happen. When Alex closes the double doors, I'm tempted to leave the room and find Sally so I can talk to her about what happened. But what do I say? Because of who Alex's family is, a man attacked my mother? None of it makes sense. We're PAs, cleaners, and glorified servants. What value do we have?

My exhausted brain demands sleep. So, I give in and draw the large red drapes of the red room. That's what we call it. Not very creative, but most rooms in the house have names or zones. It's easier on the staff. I'm sure Alex has no idea.

Alex. Alex. Alex.

I open my suitcase and take out a pair of black leggings and an oversized sweater that I love to sleep in. After getting changed, I wash my face and tie up my long black hair. The front strands have a slight wave compared to the straightness of the back. My mother always complimented the oddness of my hair.

I swallow the pain of knowing how sick she is and get my phone before leaving it on the bedside table. I'll take a nap, and when I wake, I'll call her. As I climb into bed, I don't expect to sleep, yet I do.

***

Waking in a strange bed, I remember everything from the bad date, my car, finding my mother, Alex arriving, and now being in his house. So much has happened in such a short amount of time. I rub my eyes before I reach for my phone. It's five in the morning, and I've slept for nearly sixteen hours. I don't think I've ever done that before. I dial the hospital. I know my mother will be asleep, but the nurses' station answers. My mother is sleeping and has been since I left yesterday. She's eaten a few times, which is a good sign. I thank the nurse and get out of bed.

Taking a shower feels a little more intimate than sleeping in the bed. Maybe it's taking off all my clothes. I wash quickly and wrap myself in a large red towel I could wrap around me twice. I don't linger in the gold bathroom. From gold taps to gold trimmings, almost everything is gold or white marble, hence the name the staff gave this room.

I pick out a fresh pair of black jeans and an emerald green sweater with small cream pearls stitched across the front. It's one of my favorites, but the fact I can't machine wash it means it's one I don't wear often.

I brush out my hair and leave it down before cleaning the bathroom and the bedroom. I store my suitcase under the bed, so the room doesn't look like it's been used. I'm sure the staff is already whispering about my staying here, but I don't need to leave any evidence. I grab my shoulder bag as I get some fresh red towels from the linen storage and take the wet towels down to the laundry station. I'm tempted to have something to eat, as I haven't eaten much. The omelet Alex made smelled divine, but eating with him so close just hadn't been possible. I don't see him as I move through the house, but I'm grateful. Getting out my phone, I dial a taxi and without delay, leave the house.

***

When I arrive at the hospital, my mother is sitting up eating her breakfast. I got my own at one of the nearby cafés that open at six. I'd sat for over an hour looking out the window as the rain thrashed harshly against the pane.

I had to wait until an appropriate hour to arrive at the hospital. With my takeaway coffee, I lean in and press a kiss against my mother's cheek.

"Don't you look Irish in your emerald green." She smiles at me. It's a wide, happy smile. God, she's so strong.

I muster up a smile myself. "I am Irish."

"You look refreshed." She has a twinkle in her eye—a twinkle I don't like—but there's no need to beat around the bush.

"Yeah, I stayed at Alex's last night. It's temporary, until you get out." I take a sip of the coffee as she smiles.

"So he kept his word." She takes a bit of her toast, and I see the shake in her hands. She might be smiling, but my mother is hurting.

"Why didn't you tell me?" I can't keep it in any longer. "I had to find out from a stranger." My vision blurs as the truth of the matter races across my mind. My mother might die. "You should have told me."

The toast lands on the plate. "You can't change fate."

Such bullshit. "I'm your daughter. Your only daughter. I have a right to know." I blink the tears angrily. I want to scream at her; I can't lose her. I will have nothing and nobody.

"You would never have known. Just unfortunate events landed me in here."

My tears stop. I'm staring at my mother, wondering if she's serious. She clearly is. I want to protest but remember she's in a hospital bed.

"You could have talked to me," I settle on.

"You do enough for me, Nadia. You care for me, and I know my illness has put your life on hold."

I'm already shaking my head. "I wouldn't want to be anywhere else but with you," I say and mean it.

"I'll be home soon. The doctor said only a few more days, and I will be released." It didn't change the fact that her kidneys were failing.

I force a smile. "Okay." I stay with her for a few hours, until her dinner comes and I'm asked to leave. The hospital is normally far stricter about visitors, so I take my leave.

"I'll call you later," I promise and press a kiss to her forehead.

I don't want to go back to Alex's, so I call a taxi and make my way to the gym. I need to blow off some steam, and that seems like the perfect place right now.

CHAPTER EIGHT

NAIDA

I KEEP A SPARE set of workout clothes at the gym in case of emergencies. It saves me from going back to Alex's or having to go home. The thought of my home gives me a shiver. You get so comfortable in your own space, and when something like a burglary happens, it takes that sense of security away. I still need to give my statement at the Gardaí station. After the gym, that's where I will go. But for right now, I need to forget everything, and working out does that for me.

The taxi drops me off, and when I enter, Eddie is there with one of his clients. He smiles when he sees me, and I'm happy to see him, too. He's my normality at this moment. A few other people are working out, but there aren't many around at this time. The evenings are often the busiest.

I get changed into sweatpants and a tank top and make my way out onto the floor. The treadmill takes the brunt of my frustration, and after forty minutes of running, I slow the machine. Eddie has finished up with one of his private lessons and walks toward me with a towel thrown over his shoulder.

"I wasn't sure if you were coming in today." He leans against the rail on the treadmill as I come to a complete stop.

"Today, I really needed to come."

He runs the towel along the back of his neck. "Work or the date?" he asks.

It's always work, and before he can offer me a job again, I tell him about my mother.

"She's okay and will be released soon, but..." I exhale and get off the treadmill. "Just knowing someone was in our house is scary."

"Jesus Christ, of course. Are you staying there by yourself?" His concern drags his brows together.

My stomach twists, and I divert my gaze. "I'm staying with Alex."

"Your boss?" Astonishment coats his words. I don't blame Eddie. I've been complaining about Alex all the time, and now I'm staying with him.

I don't tell him about the security watching the house or anything like that. I'm sure Eddie knows who Alex Murphy really is, but it isn't something I'm going to say out loud. That he's Mafia. It's the side of the Murphys I've never seen, so I pretend it doesn't exist. Or that the word Mafia refers to violence, drugs, and crime. I tell myself it's not like that these days. It's a business that isn't a hundred percent legit. Or, they have a way of getting out of trouble. Like the time Jason was stopped for drunk driving. There was a fiasco in the house, but it all disappeared. The same laws don't apply to the Murphys as they do to the rest of us.

"You know you can stay at my place." The offer is something I would normally decline, but for the first time, I take Eddie's offer with real consideration.

"I'll let you know."

His eyes light up with surprise.

The door opens, and a young woman enters. Eddie glances over. "My next training session is here."

I wave him off. "I'm going to shower and head to work."

"Text me and let me know. I'll be finished at six." He squeezes my shoulder before walking away.

Staying with Eddie would be odd, but staying with Alex is a minefield I have no idea how to navigate.

I shower and get back into my clothes before ringing a taxi. I need my car before I end up with a huge bill from taxi services. I stop off at the Gardaí station and give my statement. I don't have anything to tell, as all I found was my mother. They asked if anything was missing, and I realized nothing was. So, what was the person doing there? Or maybe my arriving home chased him off. The idea that the burglar could have still been in the house leaves me with a horrible, unsettling feeling.

***

Back at work, Sally is the only one brave enough to ask me if something has happened since I stayed at Alex's last night, so I tell her about the burglary. She gives me a big hug, making me realize that I need the contact. I break the embrace before I cry and start work. I have no idea how much the hospital bill will be, but I know it won't be cheap. The last time my mother was in a hospital, they charged three hundred and fifty euros a night for the bed. My private health insurance covered seventy percent, but I had to pay out of pocket for the rest. So not working isn't an option.

The day flies by with booking Alex's appointments, the hotel check-ins, and admin work. When it comes time to bring him his coffee, I hesitate. I don't want to see him. I haven't seen him since yesterday, but I'm Nadia Greenwood, and this is my job. I make the coffee just as he likes it and carry it to his office. One soft knock, and I hear him mumble behind the door for me to enter. When I do, he wears a look of surprise before it turns to impatience. I don't delay but walk to his desk and place the coffee on the silver coaster.

"I sent you your appointments for this week."

He hasn't touched his coffee but stares at me, and it's unsettling. "Why are you working?"

I want to laugh. "This is my job." Unless I'm getting fired. That thought has me wanting to be nicer to him. God, I need this job more than ever.

"Take the day off and rest." He lowers his gaze to the laptop like that's the end of it.

"I'm good," I answer and I'm ready to leave.

"That wasn't a request, Nadia."

I freeze midstep. God, why does he make everything so hard? We don't all live in a world of luxury. "I need to work, Alex." Saying his name is odd. Everyone calls him Mr. Murphy. I don't normally use his first name.

"To take your mind off everything?" he offers and picks up his coffee.

Being here takes my mind off nothing. In fact, it makes everything worse. Taking Eddie up on his offer to stay with him for a few days until my mother gets out seems like the only way.

"Yes," I answer, not telling him the truth—that I need the money.

"If you want to talk about what happened, I'm here," Alex offers with a softness to his words and eyes.

And if this had been a few years ago, I would have folded, slumped into the chair across from Alex, and told him all my fears. He's just never asked, but now he has, and the words are lodged in my throat. That old sense of trust raises its head, and I'm thinking about all the fun we once had. How he was my every thought. He broke me once, and I know I can't allow him to break me again.

"Thanks. But I'm fine." Before he can say anything else, I straighten and banish the thoughts of letting him back in, no matter how badly I want to. I need to protect myself.

"Is there anything else you need?" I ask as he continues to stare at me.

After a moment, he shakes his head, and I leave. The minute I close the door to his office, my body wants to slump, but I keep walking and get back to work. The day comes to an end, and I know I can't stay here any longer.

One of the security personnel approaches me when I'm hauling my bag down the stairs. I know there are cameras in the house, and I'm sure Alex has sent him to ask me what I'm doing, but I won't give in. When he holds out a set of keys, the tightness in my shoulders relaxes.

"Your car. Alex asked me to pick it up for you." He places them in my outstretched hand, and I accept them. "Do you need a hand?" He juts his chin toward the suitcase.

"No, thank you. And thanks for getting my car." I continue down the stairs.

"That's no problem, Nadia." He shadows me all the way to the front door, and once I'm outside, I see my small Ford car parked in the drive. After placing my suitcase in the trunk, I get in and send Eddie a text, letting him know I'm on my way.

Great. I'll see you soon, he sends back, along with his address.

He doesn't live far from the gym, which is convenient. I drive out of Alex's estate with mixed feelings, but I know deep down, I'm making the best decision for me. On the way, I call the hospital, and they inform me that some of my mother's caregivers are there visiting her. I smile, wondering if one of them is Denise. I'm sure my mother is ecstatic. She's eaten all her dinner, and the nurse sounds bright. So I take the small win as I park outside the large yellow building that houses several apartments. I get my suitcase and lock the car before approaching the switchboard. Pressing the number seven, the front door buzzes, giving me entry. The clean entryway is bare except for a line of steel postboxes and someone's bike. I clear three steps when Eddie comes rushing down the steps.

"Let me get that for you." He takes the suitcase out of my hand and continues up the stairs.

"I really hope I'm not intruding." Having Eddie at the gym to talk to is one thing; staying with him feels different.

"I'm glad to have you, Nadia." He smiles as he pushes open the front door to his apartment. The large space is warm and clean. The L-shaped couch takes up most of the living space, and from the dented cushions and the paused image on the screen, I see I've disturbed him.

A small kitchenette billows with steam from two pots. "I was just making dinner."

I don't know where to sit, so I stand close to the couch. "Are you sure about this, Eddie?"

He places my suitcase along the kitchen counter and checks his dinner. "I wouldn't have offered it if I wasn't sure, Nadia. Sit down." He points to one of the high stools along the counter. He has no kitchen table or chairs.

I do as he says and try to relax. Three large windows let in the dwindling evening light. I get up off the stool and walk to the window.

"You have a great view," I say as I glance down onto the street and see my small blue car. Traffic moves below us, and the buildings across from his apartment don't block the view to the large park where a few occupants are walking. A couple sits on the bench talking.

"Yeah, I moved in only six months ago. It's a nice area," Eddie says as he dishes out food for two.

"And it's close to work," I offer.

He smiles. "It's walking distance. Come on, sit down and relax."

I let out a breath and smile. He must see how tense I am. "I really appreciate this."

"I know you do. So don't mention it again."

I sit down and accept the potatoes, broccoli, and fish dinner. It's simple, but I eat every forkful.

After eating, Eddie sends me to the couch as he cleans up. I offer to help, but of course he won't have it. I watch him move around the kitchen, and it makes me think of Alex cooking for me. Watching Alex made me yearn for him; it showed me he was almost human. Outside of work, he could do normal things, and the fact he had cooked for me made me want him more.

Watching Eddie has no effect, only guilt that I should be cleaning since he cooked. Were my feelings for Alex normal? Or would any girl having Alex Murphy cook for them feel the same? Alex could have any woman he wanted; his looks and wealth would garner him any female on the planet.

"Penny for your thoughts," Eddie says.

Jesus, I've been staring at him for far too long. I blink and look away before giving a half-truth.. "I was thinking about work."

Eddie wipes his hands on the kitchen towel and sits beside me on the couch. "No talk of work. Now we're watching a movie."

He hits play and the movie continues. Tom Cruise runs up the side of a large hill after his son. I know this movie. "*War of the Worlds*?" I say.

"One of my favorites." Eddie speaks while engrossed in the screen.

I sit back and try to get lost in the movie, but Alex is never far from my mind.

CHAPTER NINE

ALEX

I'M LEAVING TO MEET Jason, Aidan, Matty, and William. We've run into a shipment problem. It was mentioned at the meeting the other day, but it hadn't affected us until now.

The meeting is at Aidan's house. He's remained in the family home, and it's where all our meetings normally are. I hate being here. I hate the reminder of what I've done, even though my father left me no choice.

The company is slipping out of his hands and into Frank's. If Frank got it all, it would go to Jason, who I had found out isn't my brother but my cousin. His mother was also Bratva, and my father wouldn't allow that kind of power. He had contracted me to kill Jason, and I couldn't. He wanted him dead before Frank got more power. Gilly would die next, and that loophole in the contract sent the business back to me, the next in line.

That loophole made Father sloppy. He had handed over percentages of the business at times when other investments drained his fortune. We were asset rich but money poor at the time. Frank pumped the money into our accounts, and in return, he got the company slowly, one percentage at a time. My father thought I would kill Jason and Gilly; therefore, he didn't put up more of a fight than he needed to.

If I didn't kill Jason, someone else would. But my father wanted it to be me. To show him how badly I wanted the family empire. I didn't want to lose everything to Frank but killing Jason wasn't something I could do, so I did the unthinkable—killed my father.

William is standing outside. He's getting bigger each time I see him. He's pumping iron daily now. He looks healthy. He's smoking, a habit he hasn't been able to quit yet. But I'm sure he will conquer it. I tuck away all my fears of them finding out about my father and get out of the car.

I have the same old question playing around in my mind. If I had told them, would they have done something to stop the killing of Jason? They hadn't known that Jason wasn't our brother, so I wasn't sure they would stand against our father for him.

"I thought you were going to quit," I say as I climb the steps to the front door.

"You think it would be easy." He grins as he looks at the cigarette between his fingers. "Everyone is inside waiting." His grin dissolves, and he crushes the half-smoked cigarette under his shoe.

We all look so much alike. William has all our features—dark hair and eyes. We are all over six feet, but when I enter the meeting room where the rest of my brothers are, I glance at Jason. He's the odd one out with green eyes. It's not obvious we aren't brothers; I mean, we were fooled most of our lives.

"Matty." The second youngest slumps in a chair and always looks like he would rather be anywhere but here, but if work needs to be done, Matty will do it. He's also qualified as an accountant, and so, he does most of the books. I think he's so used to being alone in a room that when he comes out and has to be social, he struggles.

"How was the meeting?" he asks.

"They had shipment problems, too." I speak to Jason and Aidan. "The O'Reagans were sending some of their men, along with the O'Rourkes, and we sent some. But I see that didn't fix the problem."

"There hasn't been a hit on our shipments before. Maybe it cut off one path for them, so they focused on another," Aidan says as he sits down.

"Yeah, ours," William sneers as he stays standing.

Jason places a brown folder on the table. I pick up the file and open it.

"A biker gang?" I quiz.

"Our intel says they are orchestrating the hits. We should send in men." I'm staring at the ringleader and turning the page. The image of the club has black marble coating its walls and the words Rose Gardens embroidered in gold across the door.

"This is their base?" I ask Jason since he's the one who brought the file.

"Yes, they spend most of their time there. Lexi controls several gangs in the area. He doesn't have full control, but they pay hush money to him, and in return, he doesn't burn their business to the ground. He's callous," Jason says.

"We should send in our men." Aidan walks to the table.

"And burn it to the ground." I thought William's ruthlessness was from drugs and alcohol, but he hasn't toned down. If anything, I'd say he's worse.

"Maybe just talking to them first would be wise," Matty says from his slumped position, not even bothering to look up from his phone. I would normally tend to agree with Matty, but ever since Nadia's home was attacked, I've been working through my emotions, and anger seems to be consuming me.

"We go and make an example of them." I look at every one of my brothers. I do have the only say here, but I respect their votes too.

Matty looks at me. "And talk?"

"Whatever it takes. If you nip this in the bud, it will stop anyone else from attacking our shipments."

William is nodding. "Should we suit up just in case?"

I nod. I'm not walking in there with good intentions and hopes. This would most likely turn bloody, but that comes with the territory.

"You're the boss," Jason says, and I'm searching for anger in his tone. He was meant to lead, but instead, he ended up being the negotiator for the Russian mob. But having Jason with us strengthens us, so I'm not going to exclude him and cut off my nose to spite my face.

"I think we should send our men in. Word will get out that they are ours. So, it's a strong enough message," Aidan says.

I walk away from the table. "Let's go."

Without question, they all file out of the meeting room. I know Aidan will have my back. That's part of our world; sometimes, decisions are made that we don't like, but I think sending a message that the Murphys themselves arrived will be the most powerful.

***

The club looks quiet, but that's from the outside, with blacked-out windows and closed front doors; any member of the public would keep walking, but the intel said Lexi was inside.

I check my gun and take off the safety before slipping it into the back of my trousers. Getting out of my car, I cover it with my jacket. Matty and William follow suit. Jason and Aidan pull in behind my Jaguar and get out. I give a nod to them as we all cross the road. My foot touches the sidewalk as the front doors open. I walk right in with my brothers at my back.

The dim lighting causes it to take a moment for my eyes to adjust. Two men who are dressed like regular citizens lead us into the club. It's buzzing with customers, including bikers with leather vests, long hair, and lots of scruffy beards that give them away. To the left, the men are dressed in a more businesslike fashion.

As we're led toward a large round table where Lexi, the ring leader from the photo, sits, I spot a group of Russians. Their serious expressions and watchful eyes make me glance back at Jason. He follows my gaze and brushes his shoulder against mine. He spotted the Russians, too. This isn't a place where you would normally find them.

I stop at the table, and Lexi leans back with a cigar dangling between his large lips. His long face and turkey neck showcase his age. His vest is loose on his frame, the tattoos on his arms faded.

"What can I do for you, Alex?"

Of course, he knows who we are, but I'm not here to be entertained. So, I don't sit down or mince my words.

"A shipment of ours was stolen from the East/West docks. And my intel sent me right here."

He removes the cigar from his lips. "Your intel is wrong."

His crew leans forward like they're ready to pounce. I give each one of them a warning look that promises them death if they dare touch any of us.

"Leave us," Lexi says. Maybe he senses his men's intentions.

They all rise—all but one, who lingers.

"Go, boy," Lexi says, and I wonder if it's his son. It doesn't matter either way.

"I wouldn't ever touch gear belonging to the Mafia. I'm old, not dumb," he states.

He doesn't flinch, and I wonder if our intel is accurate. We have never been wrong before.

"If you didn't do it, Lexi, then who did?"

He widens his arms; cigar smoke billows around him. "If I hear anything, I'll be sure to pass the knowledge along." And it's in his words that I detect the lie.

I glance around the room again and notice the Russians are still watching us.

"You're entertaining the Russians now," I state.

Lexi glances at Jason to my right, but he doesn't voice his thoughts, which is wise. "We are in a recession. I'll take anyone's money."

Bullshit. Bikers are picky about their territory. And most of us, be it bikers or Mafia, hate the Russians. They dabble in human trafficking, and that isn't an area I would ever touch, no matter how much money was at stake.

"Stealing would be another way to combat the recession," I state.

He rises and squashes his cigar in an ashtray. "I met your father once," he says.

I try not to tense, but Aidan steps up to the table. I don't have to look at him to know he doesn't like anyone mentioning our father.

Lexi glances at Aidan. "He was respectful of our ways." Then Lexi turns his attention back to me. "Unlike you."

I grin. He will pay for that.

"Is that so?" I ask, giving him a brief moment to reconsider his words.

"You heard my old man." The young man who had lingered earlier returns to the table holding a pint of lager.

"Bernard. I told you to leave us," Lexi barks, and I see the resemblance. He is his son; they have the same large lips and a slight dip to the corner of their eyes.

"I see I'm not the only one being disrespectful," I address Bernard. "You need to put some manners on your son." I continue staring at the younger version of Lexi.

Bernard's face reddens. "You came and asked your questions. Now it's time you leave."

He's gutsy. I'll give him that.

"I might have asked my questions, but I still have no answers." I turn back to Lexi, who's staring at his son, when his gaze reverts back to me.

I'm aware of the circle of men closing in.

"I told you already—we have nothing to do with your missing drugs."

"Now you have your answer." Lexi's son bobs his head, and he wears a grin.

I smirk before turning back to his father. "I never said what was in the shipment."

His face pales, and he shrugs. "It's either guns or drugs. So, a fifty-fifty guess."

I'm shaking my head. "I'll count to three." That's all I say before I start counting. I reach two, and a fist collides with the side of my face. I didn't see Bernard gearing up to hit me. I wasn't expecting the violence to come from him. I wipe blood from the corner of my mouth. The room is tense as I turn to Bernard. "You want to try that again?"

He's not gutsy like I had thought earlier. He's fucking stupid. His father tells him to stand down, but he's too riled up, and when he raises his fist, I dodge the swing and land a solid into his abdomen. The pint he was holding sails to the floor and smashes, and all hell breaks loose.

He lifts his head and charges at me, his anger propelling his movements. He's not easy to dodge as I turn to see Jason and my brothers holding their own against the other members. Bernard collides with my side, and I stumble but keep my balance. His gaze meets mine and what he had hoped was that I would fall to the ground. When he realizes that isn't happening, he freezes, and I get three straight hits to his face. He wavers and crumbles to the ground. As he drops, Lexi moves in front of me.

I wipe more blood off my face, and I'm ready for a round with his father, until I notice the movements around me have ceased.

"Get the fuck out." A gun is held to Matty's head.

Matty's hands are in the air, and no one else has pulled out their weapons. Someone turns off the music, and punters start to leave.

"Yella, drop the gun," Lexi orders.

The blond-haired guy doesn't, and I take a step toward him. "Take that gun away from my brother's head."

As I say that, I notice two more people approaching. Tadhg O'Reagan, along with Shane O'Reagan, stroll toward us as if Matty isn't being held at gunpoint.

"Did we miss all the fun?" Shane grins.

"Yella," Lexi barks, and his man obeys, the gun lowering slowly.

The gunshot that Jason fires is loud, and many stragglers flee for cover as Yella hits the ground, a bullet wound oozing right between his eyes.

Fuck.

I take out my gun and dive like most of the men do. Bullets are fired from all sides. I crawl until I hit the back of a black leather couch. I spot Aidan across from me; he's hiding behind a dancer's podium The dancers are all gone. Rising, I take a shot at one of Lexi's men, and he hits the ground hard. Someone lands beside me, and I spin to see Shane O'Reagan smiling at me.

"I'd say I'm getting too old for this shit." He rises and fires off two rounds of his gun before rejoining me.

I want to ask him what he's doing here, but I'll ask my questions once we get out of this mess. I rise when the shooting eases and manage to take down two more men. It's then I see Jason and William. I'm looking for Matty when a bullet nearly hits me. I'm back on the ground to find Shane O'Reagan gone. I crawl to the opposite side; the door opens as the Russians leave.

The amount of shots being fired soon stops, and I get up to see Matty empty his gun in a man's back who's trying to crawl away.

I scan everyone who is standing. Aidan, William, and Jason are all fine. Tadhg O'Reagan, who's the youngest of us, puts away his gun, his dad joining him.

"Is anyone alive?" I ask as my brothers start checking bodies. I walk across all the fallen and stop outside a set of double doors. Matty touches my shoulder, and I nod at him before opening the door and entering a hallway. A few offices and storerooms are empty. Three girls clutch their handbags to their chests and scream. I point the gun away from them, and they run out a back door. I walk to the end of the hall.

"Clear," I call back to Matty.

"Clear," he repeats, and we return to the main club, which resembles a slaughterhouse.

"Everyone is dead," William informs us.

"Why are you here?" I ask Shane as I put my gun away.

"We got intel that Lexi was behind our shipments going missing."

I nod. "So did we. The Russians were here, too."

This didn't add up.

"We need to move out," I call to my brothers.

Jason's on the phone and hangs up as he approaches me. "The cleanup crew is on their way."

I nod. "Tell them to burn it down."

Shane O'Reagan falls into step beside me. "You want to tell me who tipped you off?" I ask.

"A reliable source who was working here for us. What about you?" Shane asks as we step outside.

"One of Jason's men."

Shane's brows rise.

"He's solid," I say and wonder if he really is.

"Well, if it was Lexi, then the problem will stop," Shane says.

I'm highly doubtful. We part ways and leave. Matty and William get into the car as my phone rings. It's Edmond.

"I'm on my way back," I say, hoping whatever is wrong can wait.

"It's Nadia."

I'm listening.

"She left and took her luggage and car. I'll send you the location of where she's gone."

I hang up.

"I'll drop you off at Aidan's. I've got something to do," I say to Matty and William and pull out from the sidewalk.

I'll go get Nadia and bring her back. I have no idea why she left or why she thought she could.

CHAPTER TEN

NADIA

I'M FIGHTING SLEEP AS Tom Cruise carries his daughter back to where his ex-wife is staying. The story comes to a close when his son runs out the front door. My eyelids grow heavier, but I become alert as a blanket is placed across my body. Eddie stands over me.

"Go to sleep." He smiles.

"No. I'll go to bed." I don't want to take up his couch and stop him from watching TV.

I push the blanket down slightly, and he sits beside me. "I don't mind, Nadia. You can rest here if you want."

I shake my head and become more alert. "Honestly, you watch your TV. I need to ring the hospital anyway."

Eddie hasn't moved away to let me get up. "She's strong. She'll recover."

How I wish his words were true. "She has kidney failure." Saying the words aloud makes them stick in my throat.

"I'm so sorry, Nadia. But can't they do something?" He reaches for my hand, and I allow him to take my fingers in his.

"She's not strong enough for surgery," I admit.

"Maybe in time, she will be." He offers a slight smile.

I swallow the pain. Nod. "Yeah, maybe." I look down at his hand around mine. Shouldn't I feel something for a man holding my hand?

When I look back up, Eddie moves in closer. His other hand cups my cheek, and I close my eyes. I lean into the warmth of his hand, and when his lips touch mine, I kiss him back. The kiss is light as a feather and feels wrong—maybe because it would never compare to my first kiss.

A loud booming noise has me opening my eyes. Did something hit the building? Eddie looks at the front door, and it's a moment of confusion. I had been thinking of Alex kissing me, and he's standing in Eddie's living room, blood on his face and the promise of death in his eyes as he stares at Eddie. His gaze drops to Eddie's hand, still holding mine.

I blink, expecting the image to disappear, but Alex Murphy is still standing in Eddie's living room, and he's racing toward us. He grips the back of the couch, and despite his customary suit and tie, sails across it with ease. His movements are swift as he grabs Eddie's neck and takes him to the floor. The blanket that had covered me floats to the ground as my senses kick in.

"Alex!" I scream as his fist connects with Eddie's face. Eddie can fight, but I think he's as stunned as I am. Alex punches him again.

"Stop it!" I roar, and Alex does.

He reaches behind his jacket and extracts a gun, which he pushes into Eddie's mouth.

The air is sucked from the room as I stare in horror at what he is doing.

"If you ever touch her again..." Alex's words are low and animalistic. I almost don't recognize his voice.

Inside, I'm screaming. But on the outside, I'm frozen, incapable of doing anything except watching the horror unfold in front of me. Alex pushes the barrel of the gun harder, the steel striking teeth.

It's a sound that turns my stomach. "Stop it," I beg, my own voice strangled and high-pitched. Alex looks at me for the first time.

The gun is removed from Eddie's mouth. Eddie gulps for air, for logic to Alex's madness. I'm struggling with what is happening.

"Leave him alone."

Alex is still hovering over Eddie, but he gets up and stares down at him. The gun is still in his hand.

Fear grips me again. "Let's go, Alex." I speak gently, afraid he might pull the trigger if I raise my voice. Then my mind screams that he wouldn't. He couldn't.

Alex's chest rises and falls rapidly. Blood spots on his white shirt send chills throughout my body.

"Alex, let's go," I repeat.

He puts the gun away and steps over Eddie, who's staring at me with the horror I feel.

"He's my boss," I mutter like that matters. But I don't know what else to say.

"You can't go with him." Eddie starts to get up as Alex moves around the couch.

Like I have a choice. "I'm sorry about this."

Alex picks my handbag off the counter and walks to the door like I'll just follow.

I will. I don't want to see Eddie die. My horror turns to shock, and a tremble starts in my hands. Alex doesn't check to see if I'm behind him. I am and walk behind him; each step I take, I don't feel. It's like I'm floating down the steps, but when he stops on the third and last step, I freeze. His brown eyes are swallowed with darkness like I've never seen before. I have no idea what has made him stop, but I'm afraid to ask. He glances up the stairs behind me, and I wonder if he is thinking of going back up.

"Alex," I say, unable to stop the tremble in my voice.

His gaze collides with mine, and he turns back around and continues down the steps. Outside, I want to suck my lungs full of air to try to calm my internal chaos. Alex is standing with the passenger door open, and with no other choice, I slide in. The moment the door closes, I watch him walk around to the driver's side, get in, and start the car. I glance up at Eddie's apartment, but I don't see him. Jesus Christ, he must be shaken to the core. Will he call the Gardaí? Could I even blame him?

I'm waiting for Alex to offer up an explanation for his madness, but he's silent, and I'm too afraid to ask anything. Did Eddie do something? Did Alex find out something about him? Eddie's a good guy. I'm wondering how Alex even knew where I was.

I take my first look at him. He's calm; his hands hold the steering wheel with ease. He shifts the gears like we're just out for a drive. No anger shows in his movements, a complete contradiction to the storm in his eyes and the blood on his face.

Is that his blood or someone else's?

The iron gates to his home open, and my heart thumps as we drive up to the front of his house. Jason and William are standing outside, and they don't look any better than Alex.

"What's going on?" I finally ask. Why did he attack Eddie? Why is he so mad? Why do his brothers look like they were in a fight? Is that blood on William's face?

Alex stops the car and removes his seat belt. I want to bolt, but when he looks at me, I sink into the seat.

"I would never hurt you." His brows draw together as he speaks.

My mind races. I know he wouldn't, but I've never seen him so violent. "I don't understand." My throat and nose burn. My hands continue to tremble, attracting Alex's gaze.

"You can never leave again." He leans across the gear stick, and his cologne thickens the air.

"Was I in danger? Did Eddie do something wrong?"

Alex's gaze narrows on Eddie's name.

"What did Eddie do?" Did he break into my home? No, that doesn't make sense. I can't imagine him doing anything, and even if he did, that doesn't warrant Alex breaking into his home and pushing a gun into his mouth. "You put a gun in his mouth." A shiver assaults me.

Alex looks out the windshield at his brothers, who are taking quick glances at us.

"Why did you leave?" Alex asks.

"You don't need to take care of me, Alex." How can I tell him being around him is too much? That shouldn't matter right now. Right now, I want to know what Eddie did.

"Did Eddie do something?"

"Yes," Alex grits out.

Oh, God. What is Eddie mixed up in?

"He's a good person, Alex." I sink a little deeper into the seat as Alex glares at me.

"You won't leave here again."

I'm nodding. I need to know.

My mind is on a loop replaying Alex pushing the gun into Eddie's mouth. I squeeze my eyes tightly before opening them. I can't stay here. It makes no sense for me to stay with Alex.

"You aren't safe out there," Alex says, as if he can see the turmoil inside me.

"And I'm safe here?" I spit out and regret it. But how can he expect me to believe I'm safe? He just pushed a gun into Eddie's mouth, and I still don't know why.

"Of course." Alex frowns as if my question is silly.

"Why is there blood on your face?"

Alex moves the rearview mirror and takes a look at himself. He doesn't try to clean up.

"Why is there blood on William's face?" I point at William, who's blatantly staring in at me. But I need an answer. I'm getting none. "What just happened, Alex? Why did you attack Eddie?"

"Because he had no right to touch you." His words are growled. "No one has any right to touch you," he says as his gaze dips to my lips.

His answer has my breaths growing shallow. What is he saying? He attacked Eddie because he kissed me? Why? I'm not with him.

"Over a kiss?" My brain is refusing to understand what he's saying.

"He kissed you." Alex is seething, and I want to get away from his words, which delight me but also scare me. He shouldn't care. Why would he care?

I reach for the door handle, but his next words stop me.

"You're mine, Nadia, and I am going to marry you."

I burst out laughing, but the sound is strangled and shakes. "What? You can't be serious."

When I look at Alex, I can see just how serious he is.

CHAPTER ELEVEN

ALEX

I'M AWARE OF WILLIAM and Jason waiting on me. I know there's so much we need to discuss. Like what the fuck just went down. Was it the O'Rourkes who set us up? Was it because I won't marry Dillon O'Rourke's daughter? To have intel from the O'Reagans and from our own source sending us to the same club that was catering to the Russians didn't make sense.

"I'm not marrying you." Nadia chokes on her words. She's still trembling, and I regret that she had to witness that. But I don't regret what I did. If I had known he kissed her, I don't think all of the beings in hell could have stopped me from pulling the trigger. I'd spent years making sure no one touched her, and now this bastard Eddie thought he could just have what's mine.

"Yes, you are," I inform Nadia.

She's shaking her head, tears brimming her eyes. "You're crazy," she declares.

That makes me grin. "Maybe."

Even through her fear and panic, I can see the resistance. She won't give in. Not right now, anyway.

I know what might work, but I don't want to stoop so low. Yet, I don't think Nadia would marry me willingly. Her hate burns too deeply.

"Ten thousand." I fire out a small number.

She inhales a sharp breath, a fire burning in her blue eyes.

"That's the bill right now for your mother's medical bills." Yeah, I stooped really low.

She averts her gaze, and I wonder if she is wavering. But when she looks at my brothers and then back to me, she's pissed. "I'm not a whore. I won't marry you." She's searching my face for answers to the madness.

"I know how sick your mother is. I could get her the best care she needs."

Nadia blinks, and a tear falls down her cheek. "Why?" She's shaking her head again. "Why do you want to marry me?"

A knock on the window has me looking at Jason. I hit the button, and the window slides down. Before I can tell him to give me a minute, he dips his head and looks at Nadia.

"How are you, Nadia?"

"Fine." She sounds bewildered.

"How's your mother?" Jason asks like he isn't interrupting an important conversation.

"She's doing well under the circumstances."

Jason nods.

"What do you want?" I bite out, wondering why he's making small talk with Nadia. We have all known her since we were kids, but now isn't the time for his chitchat.

Jason glances at Nadia again, and my patience snaps.

"Spit it out, Jason." Why does he linger so long?

He straightens up so only I can see him. "Did you turn down a marriage with Dillon O'Rourke's daughter? Is that true?"

I won't discuss this in front of Nadia. "We will talk inside." I roll up the window and watch Jason return to William, who gives me a nod before my brothers disappear back into the house. Why did they ask me that now? Did they learn something? Was the attack orchestrated by Dillon O'Rourke? Answers will clearly have to wait, as Nadia unbuckles her seat belt.

"Am I a scapegoat?"

Jesus, she is anything but that.

"Marry me so you don't have to marry someone else?" Her words grow angrier. She sneers. "Is it an arranged marriage?" Her gaze darts across my face.

"Yes," I answer. But that's not the reason. I struggle as I search for the right words to explain she isn't a scapegoat but my choice. "Think about my offer. It might save your mother's life."

I land the low blow and expect Nadia to retaliate, but instead, she gets out of the car and grabs her bag. I watch her walk up the front steps of the house and disappear inside. I don't want to linger, so I go inside. Jason and William are in my study. Jason has made himself comfortable in my chair.

"You turned down a marriage with Dillon O'Rourke's daughter." Jason is like a dog with a bone.

I loosen my tie. "Yes," I answer and walk around the desk. Jason gets out of my seat, and I sit down.

"Why?" William asks. I have my own questions, like how they know, but I will answer theirs first.

"Because I'm going to marry Nadia," I say. No one laughs, though I was expecting them to.

Jason nods. "Nadia is a great woman, but she didn't exactly look happy in the car."

This is where it gets awkward. "I just informed her of the marriage. It will take a bit of time for her to come around."

William laughs. "A real romantic you are."

I don't answer him.

"You didn't ask her. You informed her," Jason says, but his voice holds humor.

"How I propose to someone is none of anyone's concern." I realize it wasn't a proposal but an angry demand. If they knew I'd used her mother to try to convince Nadia, I'm sure they wouldn't agree. "My turn to ask questions. How did you know about the proposed marriage to Dillon O'Rourke's daughter?"

"Shane O'Reagan was back at Aidan's and mentioned it."

Of course, the other O'Reagans would have shared all the news.

"It just made sense to say yes," William says. "That is, before we found out about your upcoming wedding to Nadia." His comment is dripping in sarcasm.

I want to get off this topic. "That was an ambush in Lexi's club." The boys grow serious.

"Not an ambush," Jason says. "It didn't look like Lexi was expecting us, but it wasn't right. The O'Reagans had an inside man who worked there. My source was strong, too. I mean, Lexi practically admitted to knowing what was in the shipments."

I nod. But why were the Russians there?

"We got what we wanted," William says. "The shipments are safe now."

I would normally agree, but something is off. Something doesn't add up.

"We need to know why the Russians were there. And where is our missing shipment?"

"The boys will search the office for any off-site locations before they burn it down. I hope we find our shipment that way."

I exhale.

"I'm still trying to wrap my head around you and Nadia." William grins.

A knock at the door gets all our attentions.

It's Jake. "Well, lads," he greets my brothers.

"That's in the basement for you," Jake informs me.

I nod. Duggy would give me some answers about the attack on Nadia's home. He better sing like a canary.

"We will let you get on with your business," Jason says.

"Yeah. Let me know if you find out anything," I say as I get up.

The basement in the house was renovated five years ago. A state-of-the-art gym, along with a wine cellar, occupies most of the space. I walk past the rows of wine I don't drink but like to collect. One of my security men is stationed in front of a small wooden door at the back of the cellar. He opens the door and steps into the small room. A window too high to reach sends a streak of light onto the floor right in front of Duggy. He's strapped to a chair. I close the door behind me, and he opens his mouth.

"Don't speak," I warn.

He nods and swallows.

"Does the name Lexi mean anything to you?" I ask as I pick up a wooden chair and place it in front of Duggy. Opening my suit jacket, I sit down.

"Should it?" Duggy asks. His blond mustache acts like a sponge for the gathering sweat. I remove a handkerchief from my breast pocket and lean forward, patting up some of the sweat. Duggy's hands are restrained, so he wouldn't be able to do it himself.

"Why are you sweating so badly?" I ask before leaning back in my chair and letting the handkerchief float to the ground.

"Alex, I swear to God. I had no idea…"

I hold up two fingers. "Shh, Duggy. Just answer my questions."

He exhales loudly through his nose. He's been here since the attack, and I'm sure the anticipation of the questioning has left him imagining how this would go. I like to let people fester. We have a habit of making mountains out of molehills. Only this time, Duggy may be right, this situation may seem minor at first glance, but the repercussions of his actions are huge.

"I don't know a Lexi." He sounds sure. It was a wild chance that he might.

"How long have you worked for me?"

He relaxes at the simplicity of the question. "Three years and five months, boss. I would never betray…"

I hold up two fingers. "Just answer the questions."

"Three years and five months," he answers again.

"How long have you been stationed outside Nadia Greenwood's home?"

"About six months." His fingers wriggle in the straps.

"I've had her watched for eight years. Not once was there ever an attack on her home. You are the newest member, and you left your station early."

A pleading enters his green eyes. "It was my little one's birthday. My wife was nagging me to be home on time. I swear to God, boss, it was only five minutes."

I lean forward again and pat his leg. "Relax, Duggy."

He nods several times.

"So, you left your station early to go to a birthday party." I repeat his words like I'm mulling them over.

"Yes, boss."

I jerk my head like I understand. "And your actions caused someone who is special to me to get hurt."

His lip starts to wobble. "I'm sorry."

I exhale loudly. "Sorry just isn't going to cut it, Duggy."

I get up off the chair and walk to the large wooden block where torture tools have been laid out. I pick up a pair of pliers. Having your nails pulled out is an excruciating procedure, and a messy one, but for the cause, I'm willing to get my hands dirty.

"Let's start again," I say as I turn with the pliers in hand.

"Who attacked Nadia's home?" I push down on his hand, with the pliers ready.

His eyes widen as he shakes his head. "No. Boss."

"Wrong answer." The nail takes a bit of force but comes away from his hand. His screams fill the room, and I hope by the end of this, I will have my answers.

CHAPTER TWELVE

NADIA

I RETURN TO THE bedroom, and I have no idea how to process what Alex just said. He wants to marry me so he can get out of an arranged marriage. I would never escape him. I walk to the curtains and draw them, cutting off the incoming night sky.

My heart won't find a beat and settle. It jumps and flutters in my chest. Each time I close my eyes, I see Alex pushing the gun into Eddie's mouth. Holding out my hands, I stretch my fingers, the tremble slowly subsiding, but each time I think of Alex's violence, it's like my body relives the rush all over again. I can't stay here, but he said I can't leave, ever.

I take a few calming breaths and sit on the edge of the bed. *Come on, Nadia, you are resilient*. I know Alex. Well, I thought I did. But the boy I loved must still be there. If I could reason with him, I might make Alex see that keeping me here against my will isn't right.

Marrying Alex was once a dream of mine, one that I would never have thought possible. "Be careful what you wish for" comes to mind.

I get off the bed and get my phone out of my handbag. I call the nurses' station where my mother is.

"Ms. Greenwood, your mother has been moved to a different floor."

Fear grips my throat. "What's happened?"

"Nothing. She was moved to a private ward."

My legs lock so I don't crumple. "On whose authority? I'm her next of kin. Shouldn't I have been consulted first?"

There's an awkward silence before she speaks. "Alexander Murphy made the request."

I'm frozen. He already had my mother moved to a private ward. In the car, he said to think about it, but he'd already started to take care of her as if I was going to agree to marry him.

"How is she?" I finally ask.

"She's in great spirits. I'll give you the direct number to her assigned doctor and nurse. They will take your calls whenever you want."

I put the phone on speaker and try to calm my anger at what Alex had just assumed. I place the numbers into my phone, thank the nurse, and end the call.

I can't let him do this to me. I'll borrow the money before I allow this. I leave my phone on the bed and make my way to find Alex.

I walk downstairs and make my way to Alex's office. Two housekeepers pass me, but like always, they don't acknowledge me. A man with a gold earring, brown eyes, and scarred skin walks past me. My brain stalls and skips before the recognition slams into me. He was at the hospital the day my mother was admitted. I had seen him outside her room.

I walk past him and turn my head to follow his movements. Did Alex do this? Did he send one of his men to hurt my mother? The thought is inconceivable. And another piece in me cracks. I spin around, only to see Alex removing his suit jacket. The ends of his white shirt sleeves are soaked in blood. When his gaze meets mine, an overwhelming amount of anger accelerates my steps.

"You did this," I accuse. "You attacked my home. You hurt my mother." Shivers assault me as adrenaline rises in turmoil. "You bastard!" The louder I speak, the more it hurts. How could he do this?

Alex takes my arm and leads me into a sitting room I've stood in more times than I can count. He calmly closes the door, but when he turns to me, there's fire in his eyes.

"How many times do I have to tell you? I would never hurt you."

"I don't know you," I shout. My gaze travels to the blood on his sleeves. "I have no idea what you are capable of."

Alex presses two fingers between his brows. "Why would you even think I would ever hurt your mother?"

I point at the wall as if we can see through it. "I just saw the same man walk down your hallway who was in the hospital when my mother was admitted. He was outside her door."

"Edmond," Alex says calmly.

I have no calm left in me.

"He was there to watch over your mother for me. He's always watched your house. To protect you, Nadia. Not to harm you."

I want to believe him. I want to believe Alex would never do such a thing as harm my mother or me. But I witnessed him putting a gun in Eddie's mouth.

"You are a target, and so is your mother. The quicker you accept I'm trying to help, the easier this will be."

I give an unladylike snort. "Trying to help. You used my mother's health as a way to make me marry you." I take a bold step closer to Alex. "I won't marry you."

Alex takes a step closer to me. His sheer size is intimating. "What about your mother?"

My fingers curl into fists. "I'll get a job and pay for her care. I don't need you." My heart drums when I think of all the bad luck I've had with jobs.

Alex sneers. "How has job hunting worked for you in the past?"

I go still and wonder how he knows I've been job hunting. "Did you have someone follow me?" How deep does all this go?

"Marry me," he repeats.

My stomach twists. "Why would I marry someone like you?"

His face tightens in anger, and I fear what he will do. I start to back away, but his words stop me.

"You never got a job because I didn't want you to. I made sure no one hired you."

I find my footing and take a step away from him. "You're lying" is all I can say, but I see the truth in his hardened gaze.

I'm shaking my head. "You're crazy." All this time, I couldn't get a job because of Alex. The knowledge sends my mind reeling. I move, and all I want to do is smack him across the face; I want to hurt him just like he's hurting me. "I never want to see you again."

Alex moves to the large golden couch without taking his gaze off me. My words don't seem to be registering. "That's not possible. The Mafia knows you are engaged to me, so you are now a bigger target, along with your mother."

Cruel. That's what I think this is, a cruel joke, but I can also see the implications. My legs are ready to fold. Everything—it's all too much. I can't bear to sit beside him, but I also know I can't stand any longer. I sink into a Queen Anne chair that's positioned the farthest from the couch.

"My mother has kidney failure." She wouldn't survive any kind of attack.

"I know."

A bitter-filled laugh falls from my lips. "Of course you do." I squeeze my eyes shut, hating the next words that are formulating in my mind. I'm torn, but also, the reality is that I'm trapped. So, if I can save anyone in all of this, why not my mother?

"Can you fix it?" My voice is low, and I'm not sure he's heard me.

"If I try to help your mother, will you marry me?"

He has no remorse in what he's asking. My stomach twists painfully. To think I have carried a torch for him my entire life.

"What happened to you?" I whisper. *I loved you*, my mind sings painfully. Alex proposing was a fantasy, but not like this. Not under these sick circumstances.

He doesn't care for me. I am just a means to an end. A way out of an arranged marriage.

"If I help your mother, will you marry me?" he asks, ignoring my last question, but I think I've hit a nerve as he tightens his hands, not into a fist but not far off.

"Yes," I whisper in pain.

Surprise lights up his dark eyes, making them lighter and making him look more like the boy I loved. Why is he surprised? He's backed me into a corner.

Alex rises from the couch and walks toward me. I'm too tired to retreat, and the only place I can go is deeper into my seat. He kneels down in front of me, and I have no idea what I see in his eyes. I'm exhausted, yet having him this close sparks a want I could never douse. No amount of water, no ocean, nothing could ever quench the love I've felt my whole life for this man.

"I'll treat you well. I'll take care of you." His voice has softened for the first time.

My throat and nose burn with an onslaught of pain. If his words are meant to give me peace, they don't; all they do is cause more pain and a yearning that I can't ever bury.

I blink, and tears spill down my face. I realize he isn't the boy I remember; he's something entirely different. "You are incapable of caring, Alex. On paper, we might be married, but being in the same room as you…"

The truth is, it's too much to love someone so fiercely and suddenly hate them.

Is that pain I see reflecting in his eyes? I'm not sure, but I don't care. Alex's features shut down, and he rises. He takes one final sharp look at me before he leaves the room, and I crumple in on myself.

Once again, I can hear that saying: "Be careful what you wish for because you might get it."

CHAPTER THIRTEEN

ALEX

S HE'S GOING TO MARRY me, so why don't I feel satisfied? I've left the room, but I don't feel content. The hallway appears longer than normal, and anger tears through me. She's looking at me like I'm the enemy. She won't accept that I have always taken care of her and her mother. That I would do anything to keep her safe. That I want to marry her.

I turn and reenter the room. She looks up and tries to hide her tears.

"You will stay in my bed." My heart hammers, and the unexpected reaction gives me pause.

"Like hell I will." She's standing, and a fire lights up her eyes. She's so fucking alive. Her words are like taking the leash off a wild dog. I want her so badly, and I don't know how to stop the hunger inside me. Closing the door, I turn and walk up to Nadia. She doesn't flinch or appear afraid; she's just angry. So fucking angry. So fucking perfect.

She's breathing heavily, glaring up at me, and I grin. Her face falls, and she opens her mouth, but I can't hold back any longer. I grip her face and press my lips against hers. I'm expecting her to explode. I'm waiting for her to push me away. But she kisses me back. My own kiss is brutal. I've dreamed of this; I've fantasized about having Nadia.

She finally breaks the kiss and pushes me away, only to plant a slap on my face. My cheek burns, but the pain she inflicts causes my cock to grow harder. I take the two steps she's put between us and grip the back of her neck, kissing her again.

Her hands slam against my chest, but she's kissing me back. Her anger is still evident and rises, but so is her lust as her kiss deepens, and when I push my tongue into her mouth, she whimpers. Turning her, I move us to the wall. She pushes me away again, and this time, her small fists hit my chest. She's conflicted, that much is clear, and as her back hits the wall, I advance, drinking in her anger and lust. Before she can think, I grip her face and kiss her before pressing my cock against her. When she pushes me away again and scoots under my arm, I let her go. I turn so my back is to the wall.

"Too much for you, Nadia?" I tease.

That does the trick. She's storming back, and I'm waiting for her to hit me, only she pushes my chest until my back hits the wall. She bundles my shirt in her fists and drags me closer. She kisses me with anger, and I love it. I devour her mouth, and her groans have me pulling at her sweater. I get it over her head, and I want to really take in every inch of her skin, but I also don't want her to leave. I need to bury myself deep between her perfect legs.

The bra is the only barrier preventing me from feeling her breasts as I squeeze them until she hisses. Her eyes widen, and I loosen my grip, knowing I need to be gentler, but I don't know how. Everything inside me rages, and all I see is Nadia. I lift her off the ground and turn her so she's pinned to the wall with my hard-on pressing into her core. I kiss her neck, and when I look at her, her eyes are closed, but her mouth has formed an *o* shape. When I kiss her mouth, she opens her eyes, and I see some of the anger has dissipated. I want to cause it to come back.

"You like that?" I ask.

Once again, my words fire up the anger in her eyes. She's wriggling out of my grip, and I allow her to touch the ground, but I'm not letting her go. I walk us backward to the couch.

"I'm going to fuck you," I tell her.

Her nostrils flare. Her cheeks are flushed. I reach behind and unclip her bra, letting her breasts free. They bounce deliciously, and I dip my head, taking one nipple at a time into my mouth. Her cries of pleasure have my cock throbbing. I release her nipples and press a kiss to her earlobe.

"I want to bury my cock inside you." I reach down and unbutton her trousers before slipping them down her legs; I fall to my knees. I grip the waistband of her panties before looking up at her and pulling them down. Her pussy is perfect, and I've never wanted to eat something so badly. I press my mouth to her clit, and she throws her head back. Pushing her legs apart, I place my tongue at her entrance and taste her excitement. She's so wet.

My cock pulses against my jeans, and I'm sure precum coats the head of my cock. I push my face deeper in between her legs, tasting her. Her hands grip my hair, sinking deeper, her fingers tightening, and pain vibrates across my scalp.

It's fucking delicious.

I can't take it anymore. I rise and spin her so she's bent over the arm of the couch. She's panting from me eating her pussy. She glances over her shoulder as I open my belt and push down my trousers and boxers. I stroke my cock, not that it needs any encouragement; even if Nadia wanted to stop, I don't think I could. I've wanted this for far too fucking long. I press my cock at her entrance but pull back and push two fingers up. She's soaking wet and ready for me. Removing my fingers, I press the head of my cock against her core.

I push into her, sinking deeper. She reaches back, and her hand presses against my abdomen like she's trying to stop me, but when she glances at me, her eyes are swimming with lust. I force my way into her until I fill her completely. Her pussy clenches and tightens around my cock, and I pull out before driving back in. She cries out and buries her head into the couch as I stop holding back and fuck Nadia like I've always wanted to.

Every woman who's had my cock in the past was just a replacement for Nadia. She is bent over my couch, looking glorious as I fuck her from behind.

I grip her hips and pull her closer, going as deep as her body will allow. She cries out again, and I don't stop but fuck her harder.

I notice movement at the door and glance over to see Edmond standing there with widened eyes. I should stop and tell him to get out, but I can't stop. It wouldn't matter who stood there; I wouldn't stop fucking Nadia, and I don't.

I run my hand along her bare back, pushing down on her spine as I thrust into her pussy. My movements grow faster, and I slam harder into her. Her ass wobbles from the brunt of my force, and I grip one of her ass cheeks tightly. She cries out again, and it's perfect. She's so beautiful. Her pussy is beautiful, swallowing my cock.

"Oh, God," she cries out, and I know I'm going to explode inside her. The room is filled with the sound of flesh slapping against flesh, and the tempo grows frantic. I press down on the small of her back as I empty myself inside her. I thrust a few more times as I shoot my cum inside her body. I'm panting; she's breathless, and before this ends, I extract my cock and spin a dazed Nadia around. I fall to my knees and yank her legs apart. My cum has already made a pathway down the side of her leg. I bury my head between her legs, tasting my cum and her pleasure. It's the perfect mix.

Rising, I press my mouth to hers, letting her taste both of us.

She tries to turn her head away, but I grip her face. "Taste it."

With her eyes wide, I push my lips against hers and sink my tongue coated in my cum into her mouth. She takes what I give her.

"Swallow," I demand.

She hesitates, but I watch her throat bobble as she swallows.

"Good girl," I say and go to press another kiss to her mouth. She turns her head away from me, and when she looks back, she has a look of devastation in her eyes.

"Was that not good for you?" I ask and step back so I can take in her body. She's fucking gorgeous. And even more so with the marks my hands left on her breast. The redness will fade, but for right now, she's branded by me. She's panicking now, pulling on her bra, and I stand there as she turns around. Her back and ass are red too. She glances at me over her shoulder. I'm waiting for her to tell me this will never happen again, but she just gets dressed. I pull up my boxers and trousers. I'm closing my belt when she spins with her head high.

I grin.

"Can I leave the room?" she bites out.

I laugh. I can't help it. "Yes."

I want a kiss, but she storms past me. She'll cool off. No matter how angry she is, she can't take away the glee that pulses through my body. One thing I have to do now is find out why Edmond interrupted me fucking Nadia. It'd better be good.

CHAPTER FOURTEEN

NADIA

I'M BACK IN THE red room, and I have no idea what just happened, except amazing sex. I swallow again, and I think I'm in shock that Alex licked between my legs and kissed me. I blink rapidly as my mind is catching up with the ecstasy my body just experienced. I couldn't be in the room with Alex after that. He kissed me like he wanted to. He had sex with me like I was a taste of heaven.

I have a sense of losing myself. How quickly my life has turned on its head. How quickly I gave in to Alex. But I have that kiss craved far too long, and I couldn't stop it. I couldn't stop the want that's been festering for years inside me.

I hate him, and I hate what he's doing, forcing me to marry him, but having Alex is something I couldn't have imagined. I always pictured it perfectly. Him looking down at me, both of us looking into each other's eyes. The way we had sex was like we both gave into a need that was a long time in the making. But, did Alex remember our first kiss like I did? Had he obsessed over it as I had?

I feel childish with my thoughts. It was sex. Amazing sex. A soft knock on the bedroom door has me coming out of my thoughts. I hold my breath as the door handle is pushed down, and I release the breath I was holding as Sally appears in the doorway. She scans the room before she walks in.

"Are you okay?" She's sincere in her question.

I can't meet her eyes; all I'm thinking about is what I just did with Alex. "Yeah." My throat sounds croaky, and I clear it.

Sally appears almost unsure as she knits her hands together. "Some of the cleaning staff said you and Alex were fighting in the hall."

"It was a mix-up," I say, and I'm not even sure if that's true anymore. I have no idea of Alex's capabilities. Yes, Edmond might work for him, but my head won't fully trust him, unlike my heart.

Sally nods. "How is your mother?" She seems cautious of me, and I don't blame her. But this is a topic I can talk about.

"She's good. Well, as good as she's going to be. I hope she gets out soon."

Sally tilts her head. "If you need a friend." She points at herself.

I smile. "Thanks, Sally. I honestly don't know where to start." I exhale a shaky laugh.

"At the beginning is normally good."

What can I tell her? That Alex is forcing me to marry him? That I said yes so he will help my mother? That I just had sex with him?

When I don't speak, Sally accepts my silence.

"You look tired. I'm heading home. Do you want me to get you anything?"

I shake my head. "No. But thank you, Sally. I'll try to get some sleep." I'm tired. Sally gives a final smile before leaving.

I take my phone out of my bag to ring the hospital but remember I already have. Instead, I send a text to Eddie to see if he's okay.

After five minutes, I get no response and take a shower. All my clothes are at Eddie's, so I have nothing to sleep in. I could ask Alex, but that drives me to the wardrobe, where a nightgown hangs. I wrap it around my body after the shower and brush out my hair with my fingers. I check my phone one more time and see nothing from Eddie. Getting into bed, I think it isn't possible to sleep, but funnily enough, I do fall asleep quickly.

***

I'm up at six, dressed, and have tidied my bed. I just haven't left the room. I'm stalling. I don't want to see Alex. I'm not sure I can face him after yesterday. But I can't stay locked up here forever. I need to get my clothes.

I get my phone and send Eddie another text, asking him if he can bring my clothes to the gym, and I could pick them up there. My car is still at Eddie's.

I swallow my fear and leave the room. This time when I see Edmond, I don't panic. I don't say hello to him either as I make my way to the kitchen. That's where I'm heading when Alex steps out of his office looking fresh in a new black suit. My heart thumps with so many emotions.

"I have to go out of town," Alex announces, and it makes me question if yesterday really happened. He doesn't seem fazed at all. Did he not buy my hand in marriage and have sex with me? Was it all a dream? He puts the folder he's holding under his arm and takes me in slowly, like he's remembering.

"No problem," I say.

He grins. "You are coming with me."

My stomach curls in on itself, and I'm ready to protest.

"It's not a request, Nadia." He steps up to me, and his gaze zeroes in on my lips. When he bends his head, I turn my face away, and his warm lips land on my cheek. The smell of his cologne is like a trigger, and I can almost feel each thrust of him inside me.

My core tightens. When I face him, his grin is still there.

"Have breakfast, and then we leave." He walks past me, and I relax my tense shoulders. I have no idea what life I've stepped into, but this life isn't mine.

Breakfast doesn't sound appealing, but I go to the kitchen and make coffee. Coffee reminds me of Alex. I don't see Sally this morning; if I did, I'm not even sure what I would say to her. I grab an apple and banana from the fruit bowl and take everything with me back to my room. The staff are quiet when I'm in the kitchen, and I'm starting to feel like a prisoner here.

I've always felt like a prisoner, but this is different and uncharted territory. I have no idea how to be. I manage to eat the banana and drink the coffee before I call my mother's nurse. I'm too much of a coward to talk to her myself; instead, I talk to another woman. I leave a message that I will be gone for a few days. I really have no idea how long, but I don't want her worrying about me. The nurse informs me that she will pass on the message.

When I arrive downstairs and make my way outside at the instructions of one of Alex's men, he's standing with the passenger door open. The only thing I have is my handbag. He raises his brows but doesn't comment as I get into the car. The car door closes, and Alex walks around to the driver's side.

"How long will I be gone?" I ask.

"I'm not sure yet." Alex starts the car.

Irritation claws at me. "My mother will be expecting my visits." I don't mention that I called.

"I'll let her doctor know." We drive to the front gates.

"How do you think this is going to work, Alex?"

He glances at me. "We are going to drive to a hotel. You will be safe while I go for a meeting. I'll know then how long we will be gone."

I exhale. "How do you think this *marriage* is going to work?" I ask. How can he expect this to work when I don't know what's happening any second of the day? When I have no freedom? No say?

"I don't understand."

The road is quiet at this hour of the morning as Alex pulls out onto the road. "Neither do I," I mumble because I don't understand why he picked me. I don't understand any of this.

Silence fills the car for a while.

"We get married, and you will live with me. I'll make sure your mother is taken care of." Alex recites his list in a monotone.

"What about me?" I ask.

He takes a peek at me. "What exactly are you asking?"

My stomach clenches. What am I asking? When will this end? Can he really keep me a prisoner? Can I really go through with a marriage to him?

"Do I get to work? Can I find a job somewhere else?"

"No." His answer is quick.

"So, I..."

"You can do whatever you want, Nadia, as long as I know about it first. Your safety will take precedence over your wants."

Fuck you.

I grit back my anger. "So when this threat passes, and I'm safe, I can get a job then?"

"What do you want a job for? I told you I'll take care of you."

"I don't want you to," I admit. I want my own stability. My own independence. I'm not a housewife. Jesus, that thought gives me shivers.

I want to tell him this is madness, but I don't think it will have any impact.

"Whether you want me to or not is immaterial." I go silent after that. I might agree to this marriage now, but I know wholeheartedly I can't live like this. No matter how fast Alex makes my heart beat.

I check my phone several times to see if Eddie has texted back. He hasn't. I can't blame him. I peek at Alex. He seems so calm, so normal.

After an hour of awkward silence, we stop at the gates to a large private estate. The manicured lawns and rolling hills that are home to a golf course pass either side of the winding driveway. At the end is a building that runs the full length of the property, with more windows than I can count.

Alex pulls up close to the door and pops the trunk as a bellhop removes the luggage. I guess I'll be wearing the same clothes every day during this visit. When I get back, I'll have to go to Eddie's and get my car and luggage. I don't sit in the car as Alex walks around to open my door. I open the door myself and walk past him with my handbag slung over my shoulder. He catches up with me easily, and his hand slips into mine. At first, I stop walking and look down at our joined fingers.

When I glance back up into Alex's eyes, his gaze roams my face before he starts walking again, pulling me with him. We are shown to our suite. It's ridiculously huge, and I take a look around as Alex leaves his luggage in the room. I search for a second bedroom, but there isn't one.

My throat tightens at the idea of sharing his bed. It was a demand he made yesterday. So this is when it starts. I would never sleep peacefully again. I pass the double doors to the main bedroom, and Alex looks at me as he talks on his phone. He closes the door, cutting me off.

The life of a Mafia man. I go into the main space. The sitting area looks like a cinema. The screen takes up a lot of the wall. On the left is a tank filled with fish. I walk to them and tap on the glass. They are exquisite but trapped just like me. My reflection wobbles with the water, and I step away from the tank as Alex enters the room.

He's removed his suit jacket, and I can't help but appreciate his wide shoulders, which are hidden under the white shirt.

"I'm ordering room service. What would you like?" he asks, picking up a slick black phone from a glass table in front of the TV.

"I'm good." I open my bag and remove the apple, showing it to him. I also take out my phone and check for any messages, but still nothing from Eddie. I'm tempted to text him again and start typing, but I pause. He needs time. I didn't blame him. When I look up, Alex is watching me. I place my phone back in my bag and take a bite of my apple.

He turns his back on me as he orders coffee and some sandwiches for the room. Once he hangs up the phone and focuses on me, the room shrinks, and the apple lodges itself in my throat.

"I have some phone calls to make," he informs me.

"You want me to leave the room?"

He waves his hand at me. "No, have your coffee and sandwiches. I'll be in the bedroom."

He doesn't listen. I said I didn't want any food, but before I can say anything, he walks away and I hear the click of the bedroom door. I find a bin beside the grand white piano and deposit the apple. I open the lid to the piano and press a few keys. The sound is loud in the room. After a few more minutes of checking out the room, a knock at the door has me looking toward the bedroom, where Alex had gone.

I'm waiting for him to come out, but he doesn't, so I answer the door and let room service in. They set up the coffee and sandwiches on a dining room table that's hidden behind a row of plants. This place is huge. The view from the dining table is breathtaking. What does a night here cost? I thank the servers, and they leave the suite.

Sitting down at the table, I stare out the window at the rolling hills, trees, and the blue sky. I wish I could enjoy this kind of luxury, but I'm listening to every sound, wondering when Alex will come out of the bedroom. Turns out, he doesn't for a while. I eat a few sandwiches and enjoy the coffee, just watching the golfers play when another knock sounds at the door.

This time, Alex comes out of the bedroom still on the phone, and he asks whomever he is talking to to give him a moment. He opens the hotel suite door, and three ladies arrive, all carrying bags with pink and black stripes.

Alex greets them with a nod. His face, stoic. The women deposit all the bags on the table. I can't see what's inside them, as pink paper covers the top.

He thanks them, and they all leave.

"I'll call you back in a moment," Alex says into the phone before ending the call. He walks to the bags but doesn't touch them. When he looks at me, I'm confused.

"I noticed you had no luggage, so I ordered you some clothes."

I'm pointing at the outlandish number of bags, but I don't go near them. "All of that is for me?"

"Yes." Alex nods. Whatever you don't like, just leave it here. It should tie you over until we go shopping."

"Shopping?" Alex Murphy and shopping doesn't sound right in the same sentence.

"Yes, Nadia. I'll let you take a look. I'm just going to finish this call." He leaves the room again, and I'm staring at the bags. Finally, I take the pink paper off the first one and pull out a pair of black jeans. I check the label. They are my size, but the price tag has me almost choking. Three hundred and fifty euros for a pair of jeans? It's not just jeans in that bag but sweatpants, blue jeans, a long skirt, and two shirts, all with outrageous price tags and all the right size. That's only the first bag.

I can't accept all this. I'm shaking my head, staring at the bags, when Alex comes back into the room and places his phone on the glass table.

"All done," he says. He juts his chin toward the shopping bags. "What about a fashion show?"

"How do you know my size?" Why is that question so important to me?

Alex smirks. "I know everything about you, Nadia."

I fold my arms over my chest, feeling uncomfortable. "Like what?"

I'm expecting him not to answer, but then he sits down on the couch and says, "Ask me something."

My heart pounds. Do I really want to go down this road with him?

I do.

CHAPTER FIFTEEN

NADIA

"W̲HAT KIND OF MUSIC do I like?"

He smiles. "Of Monsters and Men is your favorite group, but you do have a taste for Johnny Cash, which surprised me."

"What's my favorite food?"

"Mild chicken curry with chips. You don't like it too hot," he answers easily.

I swallow as the next question takes form. "How many job interviews have I had?"

Alex gets up and walks to me. "A very disappointing twenty-two."

Oh my God.

"How many of those jobs did I not get because of you?"

He tilts his head like my question is silly.

All of them. I can see it in his eyes.

"Why?" I whisper. "Why are you doing this?"

Alex stiffens, and his features darken. "You had no clothes with you."

He knows I don't mean the clothes. "Why me? Because I'm easy prey? A maid being swept off her feet by a billionaire?"

Alex doesn't seem impressed and walks past me. "Isn't that what you all want?"

I pivot and watch him open a small bar before taking out two glasses. "No, I want my own life. I want to make my own decisions." My anger heightens. "I don't want your clothes or money."

He fills his glass half-full before bringing it to his lips and taking a sip. "The last time I checked, you did want my money to save your mother."

That's not fair, and he knows it.

"I don't recall you being such a bastard."

His laughter is like velvet along my skin, and it soothes my anger for a brief second.

He points at me with the glass and walks toward me. "Right there. That look. That's what it's all for."

I'm confused. He's making no sense. Maybe he isn't stable.

All the good-looking bachelor billionaires are always psychopaths.

"You weren't always like this," I find myself saying.

Alex stops right in front of me. "You haven't changed."

I'm stunned when he leans in and presses a kiss to my cheek. "Never do."

I want to scream, *What does that even mean?*

Alex's phone rings, and he finishes his drink. "I'll be out all evening at meetings. Order whatever you want. Try on your clothes." He walks to a side table close to the door and picks up a leather-bound folder. He returns to me while holding it out. "You can get your hair done or get a massage in the room. There's a list."

"I can't leave the room?"

He exhales loudly like I'm being awkward. "It's best if you stay in the room. It's only for a few hours, until I get back."

It's best—meaning I can't. I'm sure his men are here around the hotel. Someone will always be watching me.

When I keep my hands at my side, he walks back to the table. "It's here if you want it."

I don't answer him as he goes back to the bedroom, only to return a moment later with his jacket on. He picks up his phone and gives me one final look before leaving.

After a few minutes, I go back to the bags and remove all the clothes. When I get to the final bag, which holds lingerie, I take out a black string that wouldn't cover anything and hold it up with one finger. The tiny white price tag reads fifty euros. For a scrap of material?

I drop it back into the bag and take out the sweatpants, a long green shirt, and a set of white underwear. The panties are small but not a string. I hold the clothes to my chest and look around the space before going to the bedroom and depositing the clothes on the four-poster bed. The heavy golden drapes are held back with red ties, the tassels golden with red weaved through them. The window is floor to ceiling, and the closer I get, I see the balcony. I open the door and step outside into the warm breeze. A set of chairs and a table are nestled in the corner. I sit down and watch the golfers for a while. Have they any idea I'm being kept prisoner up here? If I screamed for help, would anyone come?

And then what, Nadia? Mam has already been moved back to the general population in the hospital, and she won't get the care she needs.

My depressing thoughts send me back inside. I close the door and return to the main room and check my phone again. Nothing from Eddie. Instead of texting him again, I call him. No answer.

I shower in the ridiculously large shower and get dressed in my new clothes. They feel nice on my skin. Turning on the TV settles me a bit. The noise makes me feel less alone. I sit down and find myself watching a movie. *The Day After Tomorrow* keeps my attention for two hours, and when it ends, my stomach rumbles.

I call room service, and it doesn't take long for my steak dinner to arrive. After eating, I place everything neatly on the tray. The sun is setting, and Alex still hasn't returned. I pick up the black leather folder, and I'm tempted to call for someone to come and massage me just to have company, but it doesn't feel right.

So instead, I flick from one station to another, always watching the door and waiting for Alex to return. When it gets late, and he doesn't, I go to the bedroom. There are more cushions than anyone would ever use. So, I use them to create a barrier down the center of the bed. When I feel happy enough with the wall of cotton I've created, I get into bed. The TV is still on, and the noise reaches the open bedroom doors. Sleep doesn't come, and I find myself tossing and turning until, finally, I fall into a light sleep. My body is too alert, waiting for Alex to return. What would he do, strip down and get under the blankets? Would he try to touch me? That thought isn't repulsive, not one bit. It should be, but it isn't.

I'm half-asleep, picturing Alex, when I turn on my side and face the far wall. A slight breeze brushes my back, and I frown, turning around. The white curtains over the balcony door flutter in a slight breeze. Had I forgotten to close the door? I get out of bed and close it, then push up the lock. A noise from the main living space has me looking in that direction. I can still hear the TV I left on, but this sound is different.

"Alex?" I call, taking a tentative step toward the door. No answer.

"Alex, is that you?" Still nothing. My heart rate starts to rise as I walk to the door.

"Alex?" I call a final time. I know I heard something.

Finding my mother on the floor of our home has me locking the bedroom doors, and I walk backward away from them. The blood pounds in my ears. Maybe it was the TV. My legs hit the bed, and I spin. Bedside tables on either side of the bed become my focus. One has a phone. I have no idea of Alex's number; it's stored in my own phone in the other room. I could call room service and request something, but that might put someone else in danger. What if someone is out there? I walk to the doors as they rattle and I'm frozen. They stop.

"Alex?" I call again. Please, please be Alex.

Something heavy slams against the door, and I pick up the phone. The door swings open, and a masked man runs toward me and pulls the phone out of my hands. My scream is cut off as he presses his hand to my mouth and pushes me back on the bed.

CHAPTER SIXTEEN

ALEX

I ENTER THE HOTEL room. I hadn't expected to be away for so long, but the meeting with Gregory O'Hanlan was necessary for a safer future.

I loosen my tie and pick up the remote, turning off the TV. The thought that Nadia is in bed, maybe naked, sends me in the direction of the bedroom. I don't know what makes me pause. Is it the door being slightly ajar? The marks along the lock that would inform me someone tried to force it open? Or the movements inside?

I withdraw my gun, and using my foot, I push the door open.

"You're not supposed to be here." The man holding Nadia with a gun pointed at her head speaks. I can't see his face, but his voice shows his fear.

"Let her go," I say calmly.

He glances at the balcony door like he might try to make a quick escape. That's not going to happen. I have my gun pinned on him.

"Drop the gun," he says.

Not a fucking chance.

He glances at his escape route one more time.

It gives me a second. I have one shot, and I take it. Nadia screams as he falls to the ground, taking her with him. I'm moving and untangling her from him. She's in my arms, crying.

"I thought it was you," she sobs.

I want to take a look at the man who threatened her life, but she isn't letting me go. So I hold Nadia as she clings to me.

"You're safe now," I say. No one knew she was here. She won't stop crying. I have to pry her from my chest to see her face. "Did he hurt you?"

Her lips tremble, her cheeks stained with tears. Her gaze darts everywhere before landing on the dead body at our feet. Blood has made a pool around the man's head, which is covered with a balaclava.

I pull her face toward me. "Did he hurt you?" I ask again.

She finally shakes her head. "No." She swallows several times.

The relief floods my system, and I press my lips to hers. I need to taste her; I need to make sure she's okay. She kisses me back, and I taste her salty tears on my lips. A primal need takes over, and our teeth clang together as I kiss her harder.

The want consumes me as I push her back onto the bed. Her hands claw at my shoulders, tears continue to pour, and we're both driven with fear and adrenaline. She feels so good under me, and she parts her legs, allowing me to press my full body against her. I don't break the kiss; I can't. My tongue sinks into her mouth. I can still taste her fear in her tears. Her hands tremble as she tries to open my shirt, but I don't help her. I just want to bury my cock inside her pussy.

I grind against her until she's panting. She manages to get two of my shirt buttons open as I continue to move my hips, pushing my hard cock against her core. I grip the sweatpants she's wearing and yank them down, along with her panties. Pressing kisses along her neck allows her to breathe, and I lean back, removing her sweatpants and underwear completely. When I look back at Nadia, she is no longer crying, but her gaze is drawn in the direction of the dead body that lies bleeding out on the floor.

I open my belt, the buckle rattling, and it draws her attention back to me. While I get my trousers off, Nadia starts to shuffle closer to the edge of the bed. She's trying to see if the man is still there.

"He's dead," I say as I get my trousers and boxers off.

She's reached the top of the bed and is looking over the edge. I move up to her and turn her face toward me. She's dazed for a moment before I press my lips against hers. My fingers slide between her bare legs, and her wetness soaks my hand. Gripping her hips, I pull her down. Her head rests on the pillow as I position my cock at her opening. Precum coats the top of the swollen head.

Nadia rises and looks down at the white substance. I use my finger and rub it over the top and exhale as my cock throbs. I bring my fingers to her lips, and Nadia opens her mouth and allows me to push two fingers inside. I use my other hand to get my cock at her opening, and as she sucks on my fingers, I sink into her sweet, wet pussy. Her teeth clamp down on my fingers, and the pain makes me want to withdraw my hand, but instead, I push harder into her, and she loosens her grip on my fingers, allowing me to remove them from her mouth. She's looking up at me with wide eyes as I pull back before thrusting into her again.

Ecstasy fills her gaze as I pound into her pussy harder and faster. She turns away from me as I fuck her and looks at the dead body beside us. I grip her face, forcing her to look at me as I push deeper into her before pulling slightly back and slamming even harder. I bury myself in her and fuck her with all the anger and adrenaline that's in me. I fuck her until she closes her eyes and gives in. She's panting, gripping my shoulders, pulling me closer as I lose myself in her.

When her eyes snap open, I know she's close to coming, and I want to feel her cum all over my cock. Gripping her thighs, I pull her body as close as possible and slam into her. She cries out as she comes all over my cock, and with a few more slams, I empty myself inside her. She's trembling when I finish with a few final thrusts, and I'm breathless as I land on top of her.

I lie there panting before finally taking some of my weight off Nadia. Looking down at her frightened face, I kiss her one more time.

"You're safe," I say.

She nods but licks her lips as she tilts her head to the side, and I direct her gaze back to me.

"I'll sort it out."

I get off Nadia and get her underwear and sweats from the side of the bed. She allows me to put them back on her. She's still in shock, and I dress her before pulling my boxers and trousers back up. She's sitting on the bed, and her gaze darts around the room. I get off the bed and step over the body before bundling her up in my arms and carrying her out of the room. When I deposit her onto the couch, she won't let me go.

I don't release her but take my phone out of my pocket. It's three in the morning, but I ring Edmond. He answers on the first ring.

"I need a cleanup crew," I say.

"I'll get Jake ready."

"I'll send you the location." I end the call and forward the address and room number. I want to ask Nadia how he got in. This hotel was secure, and someone knew I wasn't here. Was this the O'Hanlon's doing? Had they kept me at the meeting so long to use the opportunity to hurt Nadia? How would that gain them anything? My mind jumps to Dillon O'Rourke. Would he do this because I wouldn't marry his daughter? It's a possibility, but how would he know where I was?

"I need you to stay here," I say to Nadia, moving her away from my chest. She pulls her knees up and rests her chin on them.

I get up and enter the bedroom. The wooden floor is soaked with his blood. I check his pockets but know they will be empty. They are. Pulling off the balaclava, I take in the man's face. He's in his midforties. His face is clean-shaven, along with his head. He has no tattoos, but Jake and Edmond will give him a full inspection once they remove him from the hotel.

I leave the body and return to the main room. Nadia has her eyes closed, but they open once she hears me. The fear is evident in her blue eyes.

I go to the bar and pour her out a small glass of brandy before returning to the couch.

"This will help with the shock," I say, handing her the glass.

She takes it, her small fingers shaking as she wraps them around the glass.

"Drink it all," I instruct as I gather our luggage from the bedroom. I take all her bags of clothes and leave everything close to the door. Once I do a final check of the room, I pour myself a drink and sit down beside Nadia. She doesn't speak but drinks the brandy as I instructed. She hands me the empty glass, which I place on the glass table.

"Good girl," I say.

Her eyes hold questions I know I can't answer right now.

"I'll find out who did this. I promise."

She nods.

There are so many different angles this attack could have come from, but the main two are the O'Hanlons, as they knew where I was staying, and Dillon O'Rourke.

Edmond and Jake arrive a while later, and I instruct Jake to take all the luggage down to my car while I show Edmond the body.

"I want a name," I say, standing over the dead man.

"A good, clean shot." Edmond kneels over him.

"He had a gun pointed at Nadia's head," I inform Edmond.

He rises and nods. "We'll find out who he is."

I pat him on the back. "Wipe down the room."

"It'll be clean," he says.

I return to the living space. Naida has her shoes on and her handbag slung over her shoulder. We leave the hotel in the dead of the night as we let Edmond and Jake do their work.

No matter what happens, I'll find out who planned this and kill them.

That's the promise I make to myself as I get Nadia into the car and make my way back home.

CHAPTER SEVENTEEN

NADIA

WE HAVE BEEN HOME for two days, and I still can't wrap my head around what happened. Alex has been buried deep in discovering who tried to kill me. I get to visit my mother, but I'm always with two security guards when I leave the house, and it's only to see my mother, who I have to keep lying to.

I'm back in my room, and I'm starting to feel claustrophobic. Eddie still won't answer my calls, and I'm giving up on him ever talking to me again. I can't go anywhere or even work. Alex has forbidden me to do anything. Even Sally is keeping her distance. When I move around the house, I'm shadowed. Right now, my life isn't my own.

Since the attack in the hotel, Alex isn't letting me out of his sight. His men are everywhere. I've seen Edmond and Jake, who had come to the hotel to dispose of the body, I assume. No Gardaí was involved. This life had its own laws and rules. Not what I was accustomed to.

I've changed into a white pair of jeans and a navy and white knitted sweater that Alex had gotten for me. Showering each morning gives me a chance to emotionally reset, or that's what I tell myself, but I don't think there's a reset button big enough for all that has happened.

I'm ready to leave the room and open the door but stop only to find Alex standing there with a box in his hand. A large red ribbon sits on the top.

"Can I come in?" he asks.

I take a step back into the room. I'm not exactly going anywhere, only to take a walk through the house to get some space.

Alex enters and places the large box on the ground.

"What is it?" I ask.

He smiles and my heart thumps.

"Open it." He puts his hands into his trousers pockets and waits.

"I don't like surprises." I'm staring at the box like it might hold a bomb.

He waits, and I finally kneel and take off the lid. I'm not sure what I'm expecting. Shoes, more clothes, something of that nature, but inside is a snow-white kitten with huge cartoonish blue eyes staring up at me. A pink collar around its neck has a small gold heart dangling from the center.

I glance back up at Alex, and he appears almost unsure. "I thought you might like some company."

The little ball of fur starts to move, and I reach in and scoop out the kitten. It nestles into my chest and purrs.

"A kitten?" I say and rub the top of its tiny head with two fingers.

"That's what they told me it was at the pet store."

I narrow my eyes on him. "It's lovely."

I don't know what to say.

"You don't have to keep it. But if you do, you will have to name her."

I rub the little fur ball, and she tries to grab my fingers. "I'll keep her," I say and hold up the kitten.

"I thought you might like to get out today."

I'm off my knees, holding the kitten to my chest. "Yes."

Alex smiles and walks toward me. I hold out the kitten to him. "You want to hold her?"

He doesn't remove his hands from his pockets. "I'm allergic."

That makes me smile. "No, you aren't."

He grins and my stomach jumps.

"Sally will care for her while we're gone. You might need a warm jacket."

I have several jackets, which he bought me. "You will have to hold her while I get my coat."

Alex removes his hands from his pockets and takes the kitten. He looks so awkward holding her away from his shirt.

"I don't think it will bite," I say as I go to the wardrobe and take out a puffy army green jacket.

The moment I have the jacket on, he hands me back the kitten. "Sally is in the kitchen."

I rub the kitten, and she tries to catch my fingers again. "Alex, about what happened..." I start, but he holds up a hand.

"Today we just have fun. Okay?" He walks to me and presses a kiss to my lips. I missed his touch more than I want to even admit to myself.

When he breaks the kiss, I nod in agreement.

"Go give her to Sally, and I'll just grab a sweater."

I do as he says. Sally is in the kitchen, where he said, and when I enter holding the kitten, she smiles.

"You're on babysitting duty." I hand her the kitten.

"So I've been told." She sweet-talks the kitten and seems happy to take care of her.

"Are you ready?" I turn as Alex enters the kitchen. The navy sweater over his white shirt is a nice change from his usual suit. The navy slacks still make it appear professional but a bit more informal.

I nod as my stomach does another dive.

He holds out his arm for me to leave the kitchen. I take a final look at Sally, who watches me and Alex. "I'll see you later," I say, and she smiles at me.

This isn't weird at all, I tell myself as we leave the house. When I get into the car and Alex pulls away from the house, two Range Rovers roll in behind us.

I turn in my seat as they follow us down the drive.

Alex exhales. "It's security."

I face forward and nod. I suppose this is the way it has to be.

"So where are we going?" I ask. Alex glances at me, and there is a spark in his gaze that really makes me curious. "You know I don't like surprises."

"You didn't seem to mind the last one," he says.

"The kitten is very cute," I answer honestly. I'm not a pet lover, but having a kitten would help with the boredom. I start to ask my questions when I remember Alex had asked me to just enjoy today, so I remain silent.

The drive feels like forever until Alex indicates into the entrance of an amusement park.

"An amusement park?" I ask as the gates slowly slide open, allowing us access. The Range Rovers follow us through and the gates close behind them. "I thought it would be fun," Alex says.

I know I'm looking at him like he has lost his mind, so I turn my attention to the roller coaster I can see through the windshield. We stop near the second entrance, and Alex kills the engine.

He gets out, and I'm still staring up at the roller coaster when my door opens. I get out and glance at the security, who file out of the Range Rovers.

"I'll just be a minute," Alex tells me as he walks to his men. A few words are exchanged, and he returns to me, holding out his hand.

"Are you ready?" he asks.

My hand feels small in his. I glance over my shoulder to see his men aren't following us.

The amusement park plays music, and all the stalls have staff behind them, waiting for us. "Why is there no one here?" It's eerie to see no one else as we stroll down the empty walkways.

"It's just for us," Alex says like it's no big deal.

"You rented the entire amusement park?" I question.

He squeezes my hand. "I don't like crowds," he lies.

Alex walks like he has a destination in mind.

"Do you remember when we were kids, and the local carnival came to town?"

I'm so aware of my hand in Alex's, but I try to focus on his words.

"You convinced me to go with you." He smirks.

That, I can believe. I always wanted him to live a little. His father was so hard on him that I encouraged him to let loose. What always surprised me the most was how willing he was to follow me.

"Sounds like something I would do."

We stop at the Tilt-A-Whirl. "Not the Tilt-A-Whirl," I say.

Alex walks up the three steel steps and onto the platform. A guy holds the bar open as Alex helps me climb in. "You laughed so loud on these."

I'm smiling now as the memory takes form. "They kept spinning us." I swear we were the only ones spinning at the end. The guy wouldn't stop.

"I had slipped him a twenty," Alex confesses as he releases my hand, and the bar is put into place over our laps. My hip touches Alex's.

This time, it isn't going to cost him a twenty. What did he pay to have the whole amusement park shut down?

"I thought I was going to get sick," I admit.

Alex's laughter makes my stomach quiver.

"I had never heard you laugh so much." He leans in and presses a kiss to my lips. "I used to think about it late at night when I couldn't sleep."

I'm looking into his brown eyes as the ride starts. "And other things." He gives me a devilish smile.

I grip the bar as we start to spin and close my eyes. My stomach bubbles and it climbs up my throat.

Laughter wants to take hold, but I'm holding back as best I can.

"You laughed so much that everyone was watching us," Alex shouts, and I open my eyes. He's smiling as he speaks. The lights overhead flicker as we speed past.

"I remember thinking, of course everyone is watching her. She's infectious."

His words are whipped away as we spin faster, and I can't hold in the laughter any longer as I crush deeper into Alex's side.

After a good ten minutes, the ride comes to an end, and when the car stops spinning completely, the attendant lifts the bar.

"Do you want to go again?" Alex asks.

I'm wiping tears from my face. "I think I've had enough." My brain is still spinning as Alex helps me out, and once we're back on the ground, my head and stomach slowly settle.

It felt good to laugh.

"I never knew you slipped him a twenty. I really thought he was just picking on us."

Alex stops walking and touches my face. "You weren't meant to know."

The way he looks at me sends my heart thrashing. But he takes my hand again, and we stop at a cotton candy stall.

"A large blue one," Alex orders, and once again, I'm a little choked up that he remembers I never liked pink, only blue. I take the cotton candy and bite off a small piece before offering some to Alex.

"No, thanks. You enjoy it." We walk past more rides, and I eat my cotton candy slowly. We stop at a large swinging ship.

"Do you want to go on it?" Alex asks.

I'm already shaking my head. "I think I'll let my stomach settle."

We walk around the park, and I try to ignore how all the staff wait behind every ticket box for us to approach.

"What about the roller coaster?" I ask and grin when Alex's face scrunches up. Even as a kid, he wouldn't go on it.

"I think I'll pass."

I stop at the ticket box for the roller coaster. "Are you going to make me go alone?" I ask.

He looks up, and I see the uncertainty on his face. I deposit my cotton candy stick into the closest bin.

"On my own it is, then," I say and step up onto the podium. I take my seat and smile when Alex begrudgingly sits beside me.

"You've gotten braver in your old age." I smile up at him.

He isn't happy and that makes me laugh.

We're locked in, and I almost regret going on the ride when it starts to rise to the top of the platform. The drop has me bracing myself. A scream is pulled from my chest as we roar down the large hill. When we rise again, I take a peek at Alex, who has kept his eyes closed and he looks pale. The ride doesn't last too much longer, and I think we're both happy to feel the ground again.

"Never again," Alex declares.

I bump my shoulder against him. "That was very brave."

He grins. "Brave."

He takes my hand again and takes me to the house of mirrors. We go inside, and our reflections are cast back to us in disfigured images. A maze of mirrors has me looking around in a full three hundred and sixty. I catch Alex's gaze in a mirror, but before I can say anything, he spins me around and grabs my face. His lips are soft on mine this time. I'm so used to his harsh kissing that the gentleness surprises me. I wrap my arms around his neck and lean into the kiss.

So much rises inside me. Each time he looks at me or kisses me, he makes me feel more than I ever have for him. I already know the boy that makes up this man, but getting to know this man is going to be my undoing.

My back touches a wall of mirrors, and Alex trails kisses down my neck. His fingers work on the zipper of my jacket, and once he has it open, his cool hand slips under my sweater and bra. He squeezes my breast, and my whole body comes alive, wanting more.

CHAPTER EIGHTEEN

NADIA

"WHAT IF SOMEONE COMES in?" I ask.

Alex grins up at me as he falls to his knees. The image of him kneeling at my feet is lengthened in the mirror behind him.

"No one will. Remember, I rented the entire park." He grips the waistband of my jeans and pops the button before sliding them down my legs. My hands press against the cold mirror at my back. Alex's fingers slide into my panties, and he pulls them to the side.

I'm glancing down at the crown of his head. "Are you sure?" I ask.

He gives me one final wicked look before pressing his face to my core. My eyelids flutter closed at the warmth of his tongue that circles my clit. He sucks the sensitive bud, and I'm struggling to stand still. My legs are parted, but the jeans are still restricting him from gaining full access. I push my hands into his hair, pressing his face deeper into me. The distant noise of the park music and the overhead flashing lights makes this moment feel like a fantasy, and I don't want to wake up. The sense that this isn't real makes me braver. Pushing his head away, Alex leans back, and I get the small amount of room to kick off a boot and pull one leg of my jeans completely off.

He grins before slipping a finger inside me while looking into my eyes. I bite my lip so I don't cry out as a second finger enters. His thumb works at the bud, which is swollen and pulsating. I want his face buried in between my legs again. I reach for his hair, but he removes his hand and slowly makes his way up to me. My fingers slip from the soft locks and land on his wide shoulders.

When he presses his lips against mine, my tongue tastes my excitement. His trousers brush against my core, his cock solid, and I want to experience having Alex inside me again.

"Be a good girl and stay still while I eat you out."

His dirty words send my heart racing, and before I can answer, he's back on his knees. He licks the full length of my pussy, and I cry out. My cries seem to ignite his greed, and he's licking ferociously. I can imagine his face slick with wetness and my core vibrates. His licks are longer, going from my clit to my opening before coming back up. His tongue moves faster, and his fingers join in, dipping in and out of me.

I open my eyes and see his manic movements in the mirror behind him. I'm jerking and trying to move as my body aches for release. When he pushes another finger inside me, stretching the walls of my pussy and focusing on licking my clit, every nerve in my body jumps, and the sensation climbs to a crescendo that reaches its final beat. I cry out as I come. My body spasms, and I'm gripping his hair as each wave of ecstasy crashes into me.

Alex removes his fingers, and his tongue takes their place as he laps up all the fluid that I know soaks me. When he's had his fill, he gets off his knees, his brown eyes darkened with lust. His face glistens in the overhead lights. Removing a handkerchief from his pocket, he cleans his face, and I haven't moved as I watch him and try to bring my heart rate back to a normal rhythm. He helps me get dressed, and once everything is back in place, he takes my hand, and we weave our way through the maze of mirrors.

Outside, the daylight feels strange as the music and what we just did is left behind. I'll never be able to look at an amusement park the same again.

Alex wins a teddy bear by tossing basketballs into a net, and he carries the pink fluffy animal around.

"Do you want to ride the Tilt-A-Whirl one more time?" he asks.

I'd stay here forever with Alex. I smile. His gaze lands on my lips, and he steals a kiss before we get on the ride. Alex is sandwiched between me and the pink bear. This time, I don't hold back and laugh as loud as I want. Alex's laughter mingles with mine, and when the ride ends, and we must leave, I feel a loss almost immediately. The security climb into their SUVs, and Alex holds the passenger door of his Jaguar open for me. He places the teddy in the back seat, and I can't stop smiling as he climbs in.

"Thank you," I say.

"You are welcome." He buckles his seat belt, and we leave the amusement park.

When we arrive back at Alex's home, I try to ignore the feeling of being trapped. "I have someone I want to introduce you to," Alex says, but he hasn't gotten out of the car.

"Who?" I ask immediately.

He grins. "Come on."

"Another surprise?" I get out as my curiosity has me following him into the house. He stops at the first drawing room.

A woman rises from the chair she was seated on. Her manicured hands grip a red leather folder. She gives me a warm smile. Her pencil skirt and white shirt make her look professional. Long jet-black hair flows down her back. She holds a hand out to me, and I take it. I'm peeking at Alex to see if he's going to tell me who this woman is, but he's on his phone.

"I'm Amanda, your wedding planner. A huge congratulations to you both."

"Wedding planner?" I ask, feeling a bit horrified. I release the woman's hand, and Alex is no longer on his phone, but he appears distracted.

"Can't we just get married in a registry office?"

"No," he says immediately.

I want to say more, but I don't in front of Amanda.

"Every girl dreams of the big day. So tell me everything you imagine it will be, and I can make it happen."

"I have some business to take care of, but you ladies work away," Alex says.

I'm a little stunned, but Amanda directs me toward the couch. "We can handle it." She smiles at Alex, and I'm sure the dollar signs are driving her to have me alone.

Alex leaves the room, and I'm not at all happy.

"There is nothing out of bounds," she says once we are seated.

This feels like a whirlwind. "I just want something small." My stomach clenches. Am I really going to go through with this?

Amanda nods and opens her red folder. "We have already started to compile the guest list."

I look at her folder and see a list of names. A full page of them. It looks like thirty people. That's too many even for me. But Alex has family and I'm sure friends. I don't recognize any of the names as I scan the list. Amanda turns the page, and this one is also full of names. So is the one after that, and the one after that.

"How many?"

"So far we have three hundred and twenty-two guests."

Amanda doesn't seem to see the astonishment on my face as she opens a double-paged diagram that shows the table planning layout. She circles one side of the room. "We have all of this side reserved for your list, so you can let me know who you would like."

Overwhelmed is an understatement. "Can we do this another time?"

Amanda's smile dissolves. "Of course."

"I'm sorry to have brought you here. I just wasn't prepared," I say, feeling bad.

She closes her folder and replaces her professional smile. She takes a card from the front of her leather pouch and hands it to me. "Whenever you're ready, just call me, and I'll come straight over."

I take the card and thank her. She holds out her hand and I shake it. "A pleasure to meet you, Nadia."

"Lovely to meet you, too," I offer.

When she's gone, I can't sit still. The idea of this really happening is all too much.

I leave the room and go upstairs but stop when I see Edmond approaching me.

"Alex is in a meeting but asked me to assist you today." He doesn't exactly sound elated. I'm ready to dismiss him too when I pause.

"Can I go out?" I ask.

Edmond nods. "I'll have to come with you, of course."

"Just you?"

"There will be other security, but you won't even see them." That doesn't make me feel better, but I know where I want to go.

"I'll be just a moment." I go up to my room and pack sweatpants and a T-shirt, along with my tennis shoes. After grabbing a fresh towel, I roll them up and stuff them into a bag. I grab my handbag, then jog back downstairs, where Edmond is waiting for me.

"I want to go to the gym." Eddie has ignored me for long enough, and a workout is what I need.

"There's a gym here."

That surprises me, but I need to get some space away from Alex's home. "I'd prefer to go to my own."

Edmond nods and presses a button in his ear. "We're moving out," he says.

I want to ask if this is all necessary, but the memory of the man trying to kill me in the hotel has me accepting the security.

***

The gym is quiet, and I don't see Eddie straight away. I go and get changed, and when I come out onto the floor, I see Edmond standing at the main entrance doors. I never thought in my wildest dreams I'd have security. I start on the treadmill and keep a watch for Eddie.

The office door opens, and he zones in on me straight away, then his gaze diverts to Edmond and he pales. I jump off the treadmill and wave at him as he storms toward me.

"What are you doing here?" he asks. He's pissed.

"You haven't answered my texts or calls."

He won't meet my eyes. "It's best we keep our distance."

"I'm so sorry about what happened with Alex, but…"

Eddie looks at me. "He came back to my home, Nadia." His voice is low, and he glances at Edmond.

"When?" *He did what?*

"He threatened to kill me. So this can't happen, and I need you to leave the gym."

My stomach plummets. "Eddie, I can talk to him."

He's shaking his head. "I don't want you here."

This isn't fair. "Please…"

"Leave now." He's forceful with his words, giving me no choice but to gather my clothes and leave. I'm angry. No, I'm fuming when I get outside, with Edmond on my heels. When did Alex go back to Eddie's? Was it after I told him that Eddie kissed me?

My head starts to throb, and the sense of being trapped tightens like a vise around my throat. I had one friend, and now he's gone.

My life is being stripped from me piece by piece, and this new life, which I'm not sure I want, is being built brick by brick.

The SUV starts to move. "Where is Alex?" I ask Edmond.

"In a meeting." He pulls out onto the road.

"Where?"

Edmond glances at me. "Back at the house with Aidan."

I sit back and seethe the entire drive. He has no right to do this. I've given in to his every whim, but I won't allow him to go around threatening people I care about.

CHAPTER NINETEEN

ALEX

"WHAT'S SO IMPORTANT?" I ask Aidan, closing the meeting room doors. I had wanted to stay with Nadia and the wedding planner, but Aidan said this was important.

Aidan has a large file, which he plops down onto the table with glee in his eyes. I don't touch it but wait for him to explain.

"I found the draft of Father's will at the lawyer's office." The will is a large file. I knew this.

I shrug. "Are you satisfied that it's legit?"

Aidan smiles and points at it. "Does it not look odd to you?"

It's a monster of a will. I pretend to examine it. "It's big," I say.

"Exactly. It's abnormal, like Dad was trying to hide something. So I wasted a few hours going through it."

My stomach hollows, and I walk to the document and open it up like this is my first time seeing it.

Aidan steps up beside me and pulls the document closer to him. Flipping toward the end, he stops at a page that he has highlighted. "It's a clause that Dad put in place." He stabs a finger at the highlighted area. "If Gilly and Jason die, the company returns to you."

Aidan looks at me for a reaction.

"That makes no sense," I say. "I mean, Gilly is dead, but Jason isn't."

"None of this makes sense. Why did he put this clause in place? Someone killed him…" Aidan pauses.

"What, Aidan?" I ask, needing to hear his theory.

"What if Frank found the small print? What if Jason or Gilly saw it?"

I sit down and rub my jaw. "So, Gilly sees the small print and kills Father, or Frank sees it and kills Father?" I ask, liking this viewpoint. It's much more comfortable than the truth.

Aidan shakes his head, not liking my theory.

"You want blood? So do I," I say.

Aidan shakes his head. "No, Frank didn't do it. I just know he didn't, and Gilly is too stupid. That leaves Jason."

"Jason wouldn't."

Aidan tilts his head. "He's a great liar. Look at how long he lied to us."

I know he didn't do it, and I'm not comfortable with Aidan pointing the finger at Jason.

"I need to find out his whereabouts that night. I need to know where he was."

I need to divert this. "You can't rule out Frank. He was vicious."

Aidan doesn't look appeased. "Just let me do some digging."

Aidan is like a dog with a bone. So I agree, knowing he won't find anything.

The door to the meeting room opens and Nadia storms in. She's wearing different clothes, and Edmond is behind her.

"You threatened Eddie?" Nadia is irate.

Aidan picks up the documents off my desk.

"Yes, I did." I wave Edmond off.

"I'm banned from the gym because of you."

I raise both eyebrows, not liking the sound of that. I threatened him to stay away from her.

"Can you give us a moment?" I ask Aidan.

"I'll call you later if I find anything out." Aidan says hello to Nadia, and she grumbles back at him.

"I'll buy you the gym," I tell her.

Her mouth opens and closes, and she shakes her head. "You don't get it, Alex. You can't toy with people's lives like that. I can't have it."

She's angry; the fire in her eyes hasn't left. I don't like the idea that she's here fighting Eddie's battles. "What can I do to make it up to you?"

She pauses before straightening her shoulders. "Apologize to Eddie."

"No." That would never happen. Before she can speak again, I make a promise I can keep. "I promise not to burn down his business."

"Burn down his business?" She's shaking her head.

"I shouldn't have said that," I say as my phone rings. Taking the device out of my pocket, I see Dillon O'Rourke's name flash across the screen.

"You shouldn't do something like that. It's not right." She sounds bewildered.

I put the ringing phone back into my pocket.

A knock at the door has Nadia spinning around.

"Nadia," I call to her as she storms past Jake, who stands in the doorway.

"Come in, Jake. Please tell me you have good news."

"There has been a hit on another shipment." He closes the door.

I sit down. "So Lexi wasn't our only problem."

"That's not the only problem. Your last shipment was found."

I open my arms. "Tell me how that is a problem."

Jake exhales. "It was dropped off near a Gardaí station. Everything has been seized."

This is bad. This is very fucking bad. Someone stealing from us is one thing, but someone trying to destroy us is another.

"The same just happened to the O'Reagans."

So, we, the Irish Mafia, are the targets.

"Is that everything?" I ask.

Jake nods.

When he leaves, I don't waste a moment before calling Jack O'Reagan. He's one of the kings of the East Mafia, and since their shipments are now in Gardaí custody along with ours, we share the same enemy.

"You got the same news as we did?" he asks straight away.

"Yes. We need to meet." I keep the call short.

"I agree, but we need somewhere safe."

"The Newgrange Hotel. I own it."

"Is five o'clock good?"

I check my watch. That gives me two hours. "I'll see you then." I hang up.

When the door opens again, I'm prepared to tell whoever it is to go away, but it's Nadia.

"I've been thinking about what you said earlier, and I don't think I can live with the idea that you would burn down a business."

I don't want to deal with this, but Nadia walks to me with a pleading look in her eyes. I rise and pull out a chair for her to sit down in. The fire in her eyes is back as she glances at the chair before crossing her arms and glaring in my direction. I leave her standing there and walk across the room to close the door.

"You know what I do."

She nods and looks uncomfortable. "I mean, I know your business might not be legit."

I correct her. "It is. Every hotel is legit."

Nadia narrows her eyes at me. "I'm not a fool. Money laundering and all that."

I want her to say it. "What is 'all that' Nadia?"

Nadia swallows. "I don't know, but not burning down buildings."

If she's upset about me burning a building down, what would she think of me killing someone? What would she think of me killing my father? So much spins in my mind, and I have no idea how to resolve this.

"You have my word I won't ever burn down a building again."

Her eyes narrow. "Really?"

"I swear." I walk to her and take her hands in mine. The memory of eating her out has my cock growing hard.

"I can live with that." Her gaze darts to my mouth.

I grin at her.

"Eddie was my only friend." She looks into my eyes.

That's not going to fucking happen.

"He wanted to fuck you, Nadia." The thought has me gripping her hands. She's mine. No one else's.

Nadia's gaze darts to the floor, and her brows knit together. "No. The kiss was a one-off."

I release her hand and tilt her chin up. "This kiss was something I'm sure he was thinking about for a long time. You just gave him the opportunity to act on his desires."

An opportunity neither he nor any other man will ever get again.

Not while there is air in my lungs.

"Once he stays away, no harm will come to him."

Nadia pulls her face out of my head. "No harm will come to him, full stop," she snaps with as much authority into her voice as she can.

This is a minor thing. He will never get the chance to be around her again.

I press a kiss to her lips. "No harm will come to him," I say.

She doesn't believe me.

"I promise. No killing Eddie or burning down his business." I grin.

"That's not funny," Nadia says, but she's softening, and I take the moment to end this stupid conversation and have what I want.

I kiss her and she sinks into me. She's light as I lift her and sit her on the desk.

Spreading her legs, I fit nicely in between them.

Her mouth is warm as I dip my tongue inside. Her hands reach down, and she grips my cock through my trousers. I lean into her hand and groan. Her touch sets me on fire. She continues to stroke my cock with untrained hands. That's something we can rectify over time. I have the rest of my life to show Nadia how to please me.

I let her stroke my cock as I kiss her mouth and neck and make my way down to the top of her T-shirt. I pull at the bottom of her shirt, and she releases me so I can take it off. Unclipping her bra, her breasts bounce free, and I greedily suck on each hardened pink nipple. Her hand is still on my cock as she hisses. My teeth grace her nipple, and she cries out. I release one nipple and suck on the other. I suck and nip at the hardened peaks. Reaching around, I grip her ass and pull her closer to the edge of the table so I can push my cock against her. Sucking her nipple one more time, I lick around it before pressing wet kisses to her flat stomach. I want to taste her; I want to spread her naked body across the desk.

I grab her trousers and yank them off. The small white panties are perfect on her, but I don't want any barriers and pull them off too. I take a moment to gaze at how perfect she is. She doesn't shy away as she stares at me with wide, lust-filled eyes. To see her so turned on after eating her out only a few hours ago gives me so much pleasure. I spread her legs so I can gain full access to her pussy. I spread her legs apart as far as they will go before having a taste of her wetness. I don't stay long down there, as my cock pulses for release. I pull her off the table and turn her around so she's bent over. The first time I fucked her like this was heaven. My trousers and boxers hit the floor. I push three fingers inside her, and she cries out. I finger fuck her until she's wriggling and pleading for my cock.

"Taste it." I hold out my wet fingers, and she tilts her head, allowing the three of them access to her mouth. As she sucks on my fingers, my cock hardens painfully imagining her mouth working my hard-on like that.

She's still sucking and licking. My other hand runs along her pussy. She's soaking wet, and I position my cock at her entrance. Removing my fingers from her mouth, I grip her neck and push her head down on the table. Kicking her legs apart, I ram my cock inside her. She cries out as I fill her quickly and withdraw. Looking down at my cock, I see it's slick with her juices.

"You want to taste yourself again?" I ask.

Nadia looks up, and when I stand back, she glances down at my bulging cock.

She gets off the table, her breasts red from the impact with the table earlier. She strokes my cock, and I close my eyes.

"Taste it with your mouth." I look at her.

She does as I say and goes to her knees. When her small mouth circles the top of my cock, I want to grab her head and force her to take all of me. She releases my cock, and her tongue runs the length, making it jump.

I can't hold back, and when I look down at Nadia, she must see the want as she takes my cock back in her mouth. I grip the back of her head and push her down on it. Her face turns red as I force as much of myself into her small mouth as possible. Saliva runs out of her mouth when I release her. She's swallowing, trying to catch her breath. But she's back on my cock, sucking it as deeply as she can. Her hands touch my hardened balls, and I'm so close to coming as she works her tightened mouth up and down my shaft.

When she comes up for air, I'm thinking about putting her back up on the table, but she surprises me when she takes my cock as deeply as possible, her hand working with her mouth. She looks up at me with watery eyes as my cock fills her mouth. She's struggling, but I push deeper, pulling her head closer to me.

She works faster, and I fuck her mouth violently, wanting to see all my cream splashed across her face. Tears stream down her face as I jerk harshly into her mouth, pouring my seed onto her tongue. As she pulls back, my cum drips down her chin and onto the floor. I jerk a few more times before pulling her off the floor. Her face is a fucking mess. She's bold when she kisses me, and I lick cum from her chin and deposit it into her mouth before spinning her around. She spreads her legs and my cock glides into her pussy easily.

I pump into her, and she cries out, looking glorious as she turns her head sideways. Her face glistens with her saliva and my cum. The addition of her tears has me fucking her as hard as I can. When she comes, she cries out, and I know everyone in the house heard her. I don't give a fuck.

They will be hearing a lot more of this.

CHAPTER TWENTY

NADIA

I SHOWER AND CHANGE into fresh clothes. Alex had another meeting to go to. I'm not settled with his promise to not hurt Eddie. Logically, I know if I stay away from Eddie, so will Alex. Was Alex right in saying that Eddie had been interested in me? I'm not naïve, but I truly felt that Eddie was just a good friend. Even the kiss didn't make me feel anything. Was it out of pity?

I'm pulling on a black sweater when a commotion outside my room has me yanking it down. I pause and slip on a pair of black boots before leaving my room. I want to do a U-turn and go back to my room when I see the two Gardaí on the landing. They both look at me, and one with a stern face and double chin approaches.

"What's going on?" My first thought is my mother. But the Gardaí wouldn't be upstairs in Alex's home. Surely, they would have waited downstairs. Another Gardaí steps out of a bedroom.

"Clear." He moves on, dismissing me.

"You need to come with us." The Gardaí holds out his arm toward the stairs.

I fold my arms across my chest. "What's going on?" I ask again.

"It's best this is discussed at the Gardaí station."

I'm shaking my head. "Is this about the break-in at my home?" I already know it isn't. They would have no reason to be entering the bedrooms.

"We have suspicion that Alexander Murphy is committing illegal crimes. Therefore, everyone here needs to be questioned down at the station."

I follow the Gardaí numbly down the stairs. I see Sally and two house-keepers being escorted outside. Where is Alex? He left for a meeting, but I have no idea with whom or where. Should I call Aidan or Jason?

"Let me get my bag." Before he can respond, I return to my room and gather my handbag.

I don't have time to call anyone, as the Gardaí watch me all the way, until I'm seated in the back of a Gardaí car.

The car shifts as the stout Gardaí climbs in and his partner gets into the passenger side.

"I have no idea what you're talking about." I grip the cage that divides me from them.

The car starts, and we follow three more Gardaí cars off the premises.

"Save it for the interview." He looks smug in the front as he stares at me in the rear-view mirror.

What have you done, Alex?

The drive is short, and when I'm escorted into the main area of the Gardai station, it's buzzing with activity. I see Sally, and try to approach her, but we are separated into different Interview rooms like we are criminals.

The stout Gardaí sits down and opens a full-size notepad.

"Sit down, Miss Greenwood."

He knows my name. I pull out the wooden chair and take a seat. "I don't know anything," I say again.

"Is your name Nadia Greenwood?" he asks.

We stare at each other for a few seconds. I want to say I don't know anything, but this will be less painful if I just respond.

"Yes."

He scribbles in his notepad. I feel it's unnecessary. The room has two cameras pointing at us. Are we being recorded?

"And you are engaged to be married to Alexander Murphy?"

My stomach curls. "Yes," I grit out.

He pushes the notepad aside and reveals a brown folder, which he opens.

"Do you recognize any of these men?" He pushes a photo across to me. It takes me a moment to take in the mangled body.

The man has a hole in his head, his leg bent at an odd angle. Everything in me shivers, and horror cuts off the air in my lungs.

Before I can even accept the disfigured dead body I'm looking at, another one is put in its place.

"What about this man? Do you recognize him?"

I cover my mouth with my hand like I can push down the horror of what he's showing me.

"You need to answer, Miss Greenwood."

I look into the eyes of the Gardaí and lower my hand. "No." A shiver skitters and dances across my flesh.

He raises both brows. "Your mother worked for the Murphys, and you grew up there."

"Yes," I mumble and place my hands on my lap. I'm going to throw up. "Can you take the pictures away?" They are still all spread out in front of me.

The Gardaí ignores my request. If anything, my question seems to heighten his anger. "These are your fiancés victims. Each man ripped from his family."

I'm shaking my head.

"This is what happens when you displease Alexander Murphy. The drug and gun trade is very lucrative and ruthless."

The door opens and a man enters. He isn't dressed like a Gardaí. "Hello, Miss Greenwood, I'm Detective Roberts." He holds out his hand. I don't take it.

I can't move.

He doesn't seem put off by my lack of manners and sits down.

"Take it easy, Leonard," he says to the stout Gardaí who gathers up the images. "Can I get you tea or coffee?" Detective Roberts asks.

I shake my head.

"Some water?"

I could use something, but I decline.

"Your home was recently attacked. Is that correct?"

Everything in me is spinning. I hear the man's words, but I can't even form an answer.

"Your mother was injured," he continues, unbothered by my silence.

My mother.

"Yes," I answer.

He offers me a sympathetic smile. "I'm sorry to hear that. Do you have any idea who could have broken into your home and violently attacked your mother?"

"No."

He nods.

The detective takes a small notepad and pencil from his breast pocket. He turns a few pages, and I glance at Gardaí Leonard, who was glaring at me.

"We had a report from Eddie Staton stating that you were forced against your will to go to Alexander Murphy's home. He also claims that Alex put a gun in his mouth. Is this true?"

My breaths are harsh, and I swallow, looking from one man to the other. "I want my attorney."

Detective Roberts smiles and shakes his head. "It's okay, you don't have to answer."

He glances down at his notepad again. "Alex later came to Eddie's work and said if Eddie even looked at you, Alex would carve his eyes out."

My soul screams, but I keep my mouth closed. Who am I protecting?

"As you can tell from all the images you just saw, he is capable of that. So, this is what I think. I think you are as afraid of Alex as everyone else is. I think you don't want to marry him because you were forced into his home. Even when you do go out, someone from his private security is with you." The detective leans closer. "Do you know what else I think? I think Alex sent those men into your home to scare you so you would have to live with him."

"He would never." The room feels like it's closing in on me.

Gardaí Leonard pulls something else from his folder and pushes it toward me. It's bank statements.

"This is money being paid to your mother by the Murphys."

The statement shows a monthly deposit, and I see my mother's name on the top of the bank statement. This can't be happening. I'm ready to get sick. These must be doctored. They can't be real.

My mother would have told me.

Gardaí Leonard slams his hands down onto the table. "Are you a safe house for the Murphys?"

The door bursts open. A man with a briefcase and a no-nonsense look walks into the room.

"This interview is over. I'm Miss Greenwood's attorney. I have no idea who this man is. I've never seen him before in my life, but if he can end this madness, I'll accept.

The Detective smiles and closes his notepad. "She's free to go."

The lawyer keeps the door open for me as I struggle to my feet. Each step feels like I'm floating. "Who sent you?" I ask when we're in the corridor. He doesn't answer but escorts me outside, where a long black limo is waiting.

"Alexander Murphy," he answers while opening the back door of the limo. The back seat isn't empty, and I pause before climbing in.

Fear tightens its hands around my throat.

"Nadia," Alex says softly, and I get into the car.

The door closes behind me, locking me in with a man I don't know. Alex shifts beside me and pulls me into his arms. I don't move, keeping my hands at my side. The limo starts to move when Alex speaks.

"What did you tell them?"

That's his concern? Not what I just went through? I push him away easily.

"They showed me images of men you murdered," I say. Alex doesn't deny what I'm saying. A fist lodges itself in my stomach. "Did you send someone to break into my house? Did you hurt my mother so I would stay with you?" I can't contain the hurt and pain; I lash out, hitting him repeatedly on his solid chest. I can't breathe. He grabs my hands and pulls me to his chest.

"I would never hurt you. You are the only person I would never hurt." His words are meant to give me comfort, but they just clarify that he hurts other people. Kills other people. A sob tears from my throat, and I lose all control over my emotions.

"I need to know what you told them, Nadia."

His question sobers up my hysteria. I pull away from him. "I refused to speak," I answer.

I didn't know anything anyway.

"Good girl."

I can't look at him. Too much spins violently in my head. I cling to the belief that he would never hurt me or my mother.

We arrive back at the house, which had been swarming with Gardaí early. There isn't a trace of anyone, but as we enter, I see the destruction they left behind as they raided his home. Imagine having children here. How terrifying that would have been. This depressing thought has me going to my room. I close the door, but there's no lock.

I walk to the bed but don't sit down. Pushing the heels of my palms into my eyes doesn't erase the grotesque images they showed me.

How could he do such a thing?

The door opens, and I don't even have to look at Alex. "Get out!" I shout.

The door closes, but Alex hasn't left. He walks toward me.

"I don't want you near me!" I bark as panic takes over.

He still won't leave.

"Stop, Alex." I hold out my arms, but he doesn't stop. He pulls me into his chest, and each time I try to push him away, he holds on tighter.

His cologne surrounds me, and I start to fight him. Alex pulls both of us to the ground, restraining my outlash by pinning me back to his chest. His legs are spread on either side of us, and I sob again.

"Do you remember the day we first kissed?"

His question pierces my hysteria. I've never forgotten. It's been a curse my entire life.

"I have wanted you forever, Nadia, but could never have you." His voice is hollow.

My heart thumps. "Why?" Is this when I find out why he just ignored me from that day on?

"My father wouldn't allow it." Bitterness coats his words.

I swallow all my sorrow and cling to his words. "Why wouldn't he allow it?" I ask, but deep down, I already know the answer. I'm a receptionist. Not good enough for his billionaire son.

"He had other plans for me. He wanted me to marry for the good of the family."

"If he were still alive, this wouldn't be happening?"

"I don't know," he whispers and presses a kiss to my head. "I don't know," he repeats while still holding me. "I'm a lot of things, Nadia, but one thing I can promise you is that I would never hurt you or your mother."

The truth is, I believe him. But it doesn't erase everything else. The question I ask myself as I take solace in his arms is: can I accept all of Alex?

CHAPTER TWENTY-ONE

ALEX

I STAY WITH NADIA until she stops crying. After a while, I place her on the bed, and the exhaustion pulls her into a deep sleep. I lie beside her and watch her sleep.

I'm not afraid of many things, but losing Nadia is one thing I can't accept, and today I was close to losing her.

The meeting with Jack O'Reagan gave me an insight—both of our regions were targeted by the same person. That is the conclusion we came to. Whoever handed our shipments over to the Gardaí was trying to get rid of us from the Mafia scene; I'm assuming to take over. One person having control over both regions would make them unstoppable.

I wouldn't give up my power that easily and neither would the O'Reagans, and finding out who did this is priority right now.

With the Gardaí out for blood and results, the problems are piling high. I still hadn't figured out who attacked Nadia's home, and Duggy bled out in the basement without giving any answers. He had stuck to his story the entire time. He was a dead end. The man who attacked Nadia in the hotel was a shop assistant at a local pet store. He had no criminal record. He barely had a record. Jake was still digging. I had hit more dead ends than I could have ever imagined possible.

The only good thing is my home was the only one raided. They had arrived at Aidan's without a warrant, so he ran them off his property.

It would only be a matter of time before they got one. I'm wondering what judge signed off on the warrant to have my home raided. It must be someone we didn't have in our pockets.

I pull the blanket up on Nadia and slip from her room.

Jake is waiting for me downstairs. "All the staff have been released from the Gardaí, and we did our own questioning. They didn't say anything."

They don't know anything. I hadn't been worried about them. Nadia was my concern. She had been an eyewitness to me threatening Eddie and shooting a man. But she had remained silent.

"All the tapes from the interviews at the Gardaí station will be here soon, so I'll go through them and make sure they're telling the truth."

"Thanks, Jake." We have our own Gardaí paid, but they tipped me off too late. I hadn't gotten home in time to stop them from taking Nadia. Now I wonder if they knew I wasn't here. This was all a scare tactic. A stretch on their part to question staff.

My security would die before they spoke against me. But Nadia, I believe, was the key target. They thought they could break her.

Eddie had given fuel to the fire with his statement about me threatening him. A jealous ex-boyfriend is what I'll put it down to. He has no proof, and Nadia said she didn't speak. I believe her, but her interview tapes would be here soon, and I'd hear everything they spoke to her about.

"Do you have any idea who did this?" Jake asks as we walk to my office.

"I had a missed call earlier from Dillon O'Rourke. I'm not sure what he was ringing for, but his timing seems off. I refused to marry his daughter, so he lost power here in the West. Maybe he found another way around that." My theory wasn't solid, but it was the best I had to go on.

"What are you going to do about it?" Jake asks.

That's the million-dollar question. "I need evidence first. Any news on the man who tried to kill Nadia at the hotel?"

"Still not much. His record is clean. We did find a living relative. She's in a nursing home. I'm going to pick up some flowers and give her a visit."

I nod. "Okay, keep me informed."

"Will do, boss." Jake leaves and I'm mulling over everything that has happened. I could ask Dillon outright if he had a hand in this and watch his reaction, or I could sit back and wait to see how he plans to strike again.

I open my laptop and check my emails. The interview with my staff and Nadia has arrived.

I open Nadia's and hit play, watching as they push images in front of her. It's hard to watch how shaken up she is, how distraught she becomes. When Detective Roberts enters, I can see what they're doing—good cop against bad cop. He tries to plant so much doubt in her mind about me. I find it hard but watch the interview to the end. I'll let Edmond go through the others, but Nadia told the truth; she hadn't told them anything.

My phone vibrates on the desk, and I take Aidan's call.

"How are things there?" he asks.

"They have settled. What about your end?" I close the laptop and press two fingers between my brows.

"No noise here. But I did some digging into Jason, and he's clean."

I don't want to deal with this, but blowing it off won't work. "I told you it must have been Gilly or Frank." Which is what I want him to lean into since both are dead, and the dead can't talk.

"I'm still not sure, but I don't think Jason is clean either."

I sit up straighter in my chair. "What do you mean?"

"I don't want to say anything until I dig a bit more."

I have no idea what Aidan has discovered, but I'm sure it's a dead end. "Okay. Keep me informed."

I end the call and leave the office. I have so much shit to deal with, but I find myself climbing the stairs.

I find Nadia sitting up in bed, resting her chin on her knees. She tracks my movements around the room until I stop at the foot of the bed.

"How are you feeling?" I ask. I can only imagine after the shit show at the Gardaí station.

"I don't know." She bites her lip.

I open my suit jacket and sit at the foot of the bed. I want to be close to her, but her eyes are guarded, so I don't push it.

"The men I killed betrayed me. They killed themselves and would have tried to hurt someone I loved." I'm struggling to explain without frightening her.

She doesn't say anything, but it's clear she's paying attention.

"This is all I know, Nadia," I settle on.

"It's a lot. Those pictures..." She tightens her eyes closed.

"They had no right to show you them."

Her eyelids snap open. "But they did. They said they had families." She swallows.

I couldn't deny that. "At the hotel when that man had a gun to your head, if I hadn't pulled the trigger, you wouldn't be here."

She takes her chin off her knees. Her gaze darts around the room.

"With the others, it was no different. If I didn't kill them, they would have killed me. Which would you have preferred?"

She tilts her head. "I'd prefer that no one died." She's nodding.

"Me, too. But that's not how this works."

"What about Aidan, Jason, William, and even Matty? Have they..."

I know what she's asking. It's one thing to speak about myself, but not my brothers.

"I would never do it if it wasn't necessary. I get no enjoyment out of it."

Nadia bites her lip again and toys with her hands. She shakes her head. "I know. It's just a lot to take in."

"The Gardaí made it one-sided. Like I'm a serial killer. They did that to frighten you."

"It worked," she confesses and regret floods her gaze. "I know you would never hurt me."

That settles me. "I won't allow anyone to hurt you." I want to move closer, but she's still struggling with all this, and I don't want to set her off, so I stay put.

"Will you hurt Eddie?"

"Why would I?" I ask. Like I don't know he reported me.

"He reported you to the Gardaí."

I nod. "I gave you my word that I wouldn't hurt him, and I won't."

Only for Nadia; otherwise, he would be a dead man walking. I would have had him clipped a long time ago.

"Aren't you worried?" she asks.

She's settled a bit more, and I move closer to her, taking one of her hands in mine. "No." I smile at her. "Now that you're okay, I'm no longer worried."

Her eyes lighten. "Aren't you worried about what you did to him? You could get in serious trouble."

Her concern is charming. "There are no witnesses."

"I was there," she says.

"Are you going to back his story?" I ask, already knowing she won't.

Her eyes widen. "Of course not."

I smile. "I know."

"I just need time." Nadia looks down at our hands.

I don't want her to spend her time up here thinking too much. "How is your kitten?" I ask.

"I don't know. I haven't checked on her."

I release her hand. "Why don't you check on her? And maybe visit your mother."

The mention of her mother causes her shoulders to stiffen. When the Gardaí showed her bank statements, she looked bewildered. Her mother had hidden a lot from her, and that's something she needs to resolve.

"Yeah, I need to talk to my mother." She's watching me.

"I'll get Edmond to take you."

She climbs off the bed, and when she is standing, I want to hug her, but she wraps her arms around herself. I don't want to come across too forcefully, so I push my hands into my pockets.

"Have you thought of a name for the kitten?" I try to distract her.

"I'm still thinking," she settles on.

"Maybe Marcella?" I pull a name out of my head.

Nadia's nose scrunches up, and I want to kiss her, but I restrain myself.

"That's a horrible name," she declares.

"That was my grandmother's name."

She looks horrified. "I didn't know..."

"I'm joking."

Her gaze widens in surprise, and she half laughs, which is nice. "You're terrible."

I can't argue with that.

I remove my hands from my pockets and touch her shoulder as she moves past me. "I'm always here, Nadia." I want to remind her she has nothing to fear from me, but I don't want to beat a dead horse.

"I know."

I take my hand off her shoulder and let her go. I'll be here when she gets back from visiting her mother. I'm sure she will need company after the conversation that will take place. I am curious why her mother kept the payments my father made, and I continued to make, a secret.

CHAPTER TWENTY-TWO

NADIA

I DON'T SPEND LONG with the kitten. My mind is on my mother. I have so much to ask her. I could have asked Alex, but I want to hear her explanation first. I've spent so much of my life paying for her medical care, and to find out I didn't have to doesn't make sense. I hope she tells me it isn't true. But deep down I know it is. Those bank statements weren't forged. It wouldn't make sense for the Gardaí to show me forged documents. It doesn't make sense for my mother to hide the truth either. But she did, and I want to know why.

Edmond drives me to the hospital just like Alex had promised. We are followed by two more SUVs. The security team exits their vehicles and escort us into the hospital. Only Edmond takes the elevator with me to my mother's floor.

No music plays, and there are no other occupants in the elevator, so the silence between Edmond and me is uncomfortable. When the doors open, I pull my bag higher onto my shoulder and step into the long corridor, which isn't like the rest of the hospital. This area is quieter, and each private room has its doors closed. When I reach my mother's door, I pause.

"You can't come in," I say to Edmond without looking at him. How would I explain security to my mother?

"I'll wait outside," he says.

I open the door, and my mother is sitting up in bed doing a crossword puzzle. The minute she sees me, she smiles, but her lips thin out when I don't smile back.

"Is everything alright, dear?"

"Of course." I walk to the side of her bed and place a kiss on her forehead. "How are you feeling?" I ask before sitting down and letting my bag slip to the floor.

"You don't seem happy." She closes her puzzle, and her serious expression has me preparing myself to ask the hard questions.

"Why didn't you tell me the Murphys gave you money?"

Her gaze is steady. "I knew he would eventually tell you."

Her answer is her confession, and I don't understand. I don't correct her and tell her that Alex didn't tell me, but I'm not about to say that the Gardaí were the ones who showed me her bank statements. How did they even get them? Was that legal?

"Why? Why hide this from me?"

"I didn't want to tell you. You were so proud taking care of me, and I didn't want to take that away from you." My mother's eyes plead with me to understand.

I don't understand.

"All the money is still there and will be yours when I'm gone."

"I don't care about the money. It's the lies," I grit out.

"White lies," My mother responds and reaches for my hand. I allow her to take it. "Nadia, when I got sick, you stepped in, and I felt like it gave you a purpose. Or control over the situation. I wanted to tell you, but you were happy."

Happy working a job I hated? But as I look into my mother's eyes, I see she feels what she is saying is the truth. I hadn't exactly been honest with her anyway. I never told her how miserable working for Alex was making me.

"You should have told me." Just like her illness. I wonder what else she isn't being truthful about. "Anything else you want to share? Any more white lies?"

My mother removes her hand from mine, and her gaze darts away.

My stomach plummets. I didn't really expect her to have any other secrets. "Mother," I warn.

She looks at me. "The burglary," she starts. "It was my own fault."

I'm shaking my head. "No, it wasn't. Don't blame yourself because you left the window open."

Guilt swims in her gaze. "There was no burglary, love. I lost my balance and banged my head, and instead of worrying you, I just thought it would be easier to say someone broke in than have you know it was my health that caused the fall."

It feels like someone has punched me in the stomach, and I'm glancing over my shoulder at the door. Edmond is right outside. If he hears my mother made the whole thing up, would he tell Alex?

"Oh my God." I sink back into the chair.

"It was silly of me. But at the time, I thought if you knew how sick I was…"

"You didn't think for a second the doctors would have told me?" I want to fight with her. I want her to see how stupid she is for making up such a story. Her gaze grows watery, and I exhale.

"I did it all to protect you." She reaches for my hand again.

I'm focused on the age spots and remember her failing kidneys. "Did you give a statement to the Gardaí?"

She nods. "I said I saw nothing. So there is nothing to pursue."

My mother: a law breaker. Lying to the Gardaí? It isn't something I would have thought her capable of.

"I'm sorry," she repeats.

"What if the Gardaí don't drop the case? What if Alex doesn't?" I say and there lies my true fear. At what end will Alex go to find out who supposedly broke into our home? If my mother had been honest, I wouldn't be getting ready to marry Alex.

"The Gardaí and Alex have better things to do with their time," she concludes.

She's right, they do. More than chase ghosts or an echo in a well. God, I have no idea what the implications of this will be. Would Alex call off the wedding? That thought gives me shivers, and I realize I don't want to lose him again.

"You can't tell Alex or the Gardaí the truth," I finally say.

Mam nods her head. "I know." She's stern in her answer.

"Now, tell me how you are." She's as eager as I am to change the topic. I'm not ready to forget it. She has lied so much; her reasoning is sound to her, but not me. Because she is sick, I tell her about the kitten that Alex got me. I haven't told her about the wedding, as I'm not sure what to say, so I stick to the truths about going to the amusement park and the kitten. My mother is delighted that Alex and I are getting on so well, and the guilt is lifted from her gaze as she smiles.

When I leave, I keep glancing at Edmond, wondering if he heard anything. I doubt it, but it doesn't stop the thoughts from spinning in my head as he takes me directly back to Alex's.

On returning, I find Sally in the kitchen with the kitten in her arms. "Do I have to give her back?" she asks with a smile.

I drop my handbag onto the counter. "No." I rub the kitten's head. "I have to name her."

"You're a cutie," Sally says to the kitten.

I'm still struggling with naming her. Maybe it's because when I do, the attachment will grow. I really don't know why I am hesitating.

"Any ideas for a name?" I ask Sally.

She looks up at me. "I've been calling her Blue to be honest, because of her big blue eyes."

"Blue it is."

Sally smiles. "It suits her."

I clear my throat as I prepare to ask Sally my next question. I wait for one of the housekeepers, who has entered the kitchen, to leave. She grabs cleaning supplies from a closet and passes us with a brief nod to Sally.

"Would you come with me to pick out my dress?" I ask.

Sally continues to rub Blue's head with two fingers. "I heard you got engaged. Congratulations." She looks at my bare fingers, and I'm tempted to hide my hands but don't. Alex hasn't given me a ring.

"Yeah, so I need to pick out a dress."

She forgets my fingers and reaches for my shoulder while balancing Blue in her other arm. "I'd be delighted."

"How was your mother?" Alex steps into the kitchen, and I pause.

My stomach flip-flops like it always does when I see him. "She's doing great." Which is the truth. She didn't look as pale as before. "Thank you for the care you are getting her," I say.

He waves his hand in the air like it's no big deal, but it is.

"As long as she is getting better, that's all that matters."

There is a silence as Sally watches us with a slight smile on her face.

"I've asked Sally to come and help me pick out my wedding dress," I blurt out.

Alex's brown eyes lighten, and his lip tugs up. "That's great. Thank you, Sally." He seems genuinely happy.

"My pleasure." Sally returns his smile.

"Speaking of the wedding," I start. "The wedding planner will return shortly. We need to get all the details ironed out."

I'm wondering if Alex will stay around this time.

"I'll be with you. I've cleared my appointments for the remainder of the day."

"I'd better shower and change."

"You look fine as you are," Alex says.

I take Blue from Sally to give my hands something to do. "I'll just freshen up." The guilt of my mother's confession is rising like a tide inside me. I keep asking myself the same question: would Alex call off the wedding if he knew? And the thought I keep coming to is, I don't want this to end between us.

CHAPTER TWENTY-THREE

NADIA

AMANDA, THE WEDDING PLANNER, arrives, and we sit down in the front drawing room to go through the wedding plans. As promised, Alex stays with me through it all.

"I have the florist, cake maker, and chef all ready to meet with you and go through everything." Amanda crosses her legs and smiles at Alex and me as we sit beside each other on the couch.

"That all sounds great," Alex says.

"So, about your guest list..." Amanda focuses on me.

This is uncomfortable. "My mother and Sally." I don't look to Alex to see his reaction.

Amanda's eyes widen. "That's great." She opens her red folder and writes down the two names alongside Alex's hundreds. "I will have all these appointments set up for tomorrow, as I know we are on a tight deadline."

"That's great, Amanda. Thank you."

A tight deadline? I never asked when the wedding was. "When is the wedding?" I turn to Alex as I speak.

"One week from today."

"One week," I repeat, wondering if I heard him correctly.

"We can make this work. There's no need to worry. I'll take care of everything," Amanda injects. "Your dress fitting is also scheduled for tomorrow. Once I set up the meetings with everyone else, I'll send you the appointment times."

One week. That's so soon. My head spins as Amanda talks about seating arrangements as if she didn't just drop a bomb. I have no input. Because I don't know any of these people, Alex takes over. He is very precise about where everyone sits.

"The church and the priest are booked. So, I think that's all." Amanda closes her folder. "I have a lot of work to do." She's smiling as she stands up.

Alex rises and I do, too. We take turns shaking Amanda's hand, and Alex walks her out, leaving me in the drawing room. My mind is spinning. In one week, I'll be a married woman.

"Amanda is one of the finest wedding planners in the country. You have nothing to worry about," Alex says as he returns to the room.

"I'm sure she is."

Alex walks to me and my heart hammers. Will he always have such an effect on me? He takes my hand in his, raises it to his mouth, and presses a kiss to it that lights me on fire.

With his free hand, he reaches into his pocket and extracts a ring. The band is encrusted with diamonds, and they decorate the obscene diamond in the center. I stand there staring at the ring as he holds it out to me.

"It's beautiful," I whisper as my throat tightens. I want to hit pause, but Alex takes my left hand and places the ring on my ring finger. "I knew it would look perfect on you."

The ring fits, but it feels heavy on my finger. I stretch my fingers out and appreciate the stunning piece of jewelry.

"A beautiful ring for a beautiful woman."

I gaze up at him, a bit speechless.

"I don't know what to say."

His laughter sends my stomach fluttering.

"Just say yes."

For the first time, Alex's gaze is vulnerable like this is really my opportunity to say no.

I'm looking up into his gaze, knowing I love Alex Murphy. I always have and always will.

"Yes."

He grips my face and kisses me tenderly. When he breaks the kiss, he doesn't release my face. "Thank you." His words are heavy, and I feel the weight of them all the way down to my toes.

When he releases my face, he takes my hand and leads me from the drawing room. I keep glancing at the ring as we climb the stairs, but I'm paying attention when Alex opens the door to his bedroom. I've seen it before while the housekeepers cleaned it, but being brought up here by Alex gives the large room a different feel.

The queen-size bed is inviting with soft blue and gold coverings. The windows line the far wall giving Alex a view of the gardens below.

He releases my hand and locks the door. "The only thing I want you to wear is the ring."

I swallow as Alex turns to me while removing his suit jacket.

"I want to enjoy every inch of your body." His jacket hits the ground as he pulls off his tie. "Do you understand, Nadia? I want to fuck."

I tighten my legs together. Alex's tie lands on the floor, and he starts unbuttoning his shirt.

I grab the hem of my black jumper and pull it over my head. His promise of fucking me has fire pouring through my veins.

He smirks. "Good girl."

I remove my sweater as Alex takes off his shirt. It's the first time I can take in his glorious chest completely. Muscles bunch together as he opens the buckle of his belt. He's toned and muscular in all the right places. I unclip my bra. My nipples are already hardened, and Alex drinks them in as he kicks off his shoes. I repeat his action and take off my own. He watches me so closely. He removes his socks, and then his trousers and boxers are brushed aside.

I've stopped as I take in every inch of his flesh. He's a god. Carved with perfection. His large erection makes me nervous when I think of how big it was in my mouth, how hard it felt to try to take all of him. I greedily sucked deep on his cock, wanting to please him.

I open the button of my trousers and remove the rest of my clothes. As he requested, I'm standing with just my engagement ring on.

"Perfection," he declares as he walks to the bedside table and opens a drawer. He removes a bottle that looks like it's filled with oil. He leaves it on the table top, and I'm wondering if he's going to give me a massage. He stays at the bedside, and with one hooked finger, he calls me over. "Come here."

As I walk to him, I can feel the wetness between my legs, and once I reach him, he sinks to his knees and kisses the flesh below my belly button. I suck in my abdomen at the contact but exhale loudly as he kisses my pussy. He looks up at me before his tongue flicks out and licks the bud, which is already aching. My hands land on his shoulders, and he leans back, looking up at me. His hand glides along the inside of my leg and stops right outside my entrance.

"I'm going to claim every single inch of you," he declares before sliding a finger inside me. My eyes flutter closed.

"Look at me, Nadia."

I do, and his devilish grin has me wiggling as a second finger is pushed inside me.

"Good girl. Keep watching."

I keep my gaze on his lust-filled eyes as he sinks a third finger inside me. My legs spread a little more, and he pushes his free hand against my stomach, pushing me back onto the bed. His fingers slip free from my pussy, and he stands. "Roll onto your stomach."

Without question, I do as he says, but I'm still trying to watch him as he picks up the oil bottle from the bedside table. He unscrews the lid and turns to me. His free hand wraps around his huge cock, and he strokes it a few times before releasing it.

He watches me as he pours oil into his hand. I don't expect the substance to be rubbed along my anus. The surprise of the cool liquid has me tensing. Alex pours more into his hand and rubs it in slow circles along my anus. I'm clenching as the tip of his finger enters, but he stops, putting the bottle of oil back onto the table.

"Turn around."

I do, and he climbs back up on the bed and places kisses along my stomach. When he reaches my neck, he looks into my eyes. There's a long pause, and my heart hammers, but he doesn't say anything, only presses his lips against mine. His kiss is soft, but I'm hungry for him and sink my tongue into his mouth; the tender kiss turns intense as his tongue dances with mine. His cock rests on my stomach, and more wetness floods between my legs.

My ass tingles from the oil he rubbed on it; the sensation isn't unpleasant, but I'm wondering what he did that for. When his teeth graze my lips, my thoughts scatter. He moves off me and sits up against the headboard at the top of the bed.

Tapping either side of him, he calls me up. "Sit on my cock."

His words should revolt me. They're so vulgar. But I'm clawing my way up to him and placing my legs on either side of him. He's holding his cock, and I position my entrance just over the swollen head. His hands leave his cock, and he grabs my hips with such force that I couldn't fight even if I wanted to. He pulls me fully down on him until he fills me completely.

My eyes flutter closed again until a hand grips my throat gently. "Look at me."

I open my eyes and rock back and forth, riding his cock. With his hand still around my throat, he pulls me close to him. His hips take over grinding up and down into me. His other hand grabs my ass before he runs a finger along my anus. Once again, I notice how the sensation isn't unpleasant. Just different. I move with his hips, slowly going up and down on his cock. The tip of his finger dips inside my ass, and I let out a long breath.

"That nice?" he asks with glee in his voice.

He pushes his cock harder into me at the same time his finger enters my ass.

"Yes." I'm breathless, swimming in ecstasy.

He continues to fuck my pussy as his finger glides in and out of my ass with ease. I'm full of pleasure bubbling and rising. His hand around my throat tightens, and he pushes back slightly to look at me. He stops grinding his hips and plays with my ass. The feeling is so new, so wrong but right. Without realizing, I'm sitting down on his finger, wanting more. So much more. When he removes his finger, my body feels the loss, and when he extracts his cock from my pussy, it throbs for more.

Grabbing my thighs, he drags me closer to him until my breasts are in his face. Lifting his knees slightly, he reaches down and places his cock at my anus. The head swells along the opening, and it's not like his finger; it's too big.

His mouth takes one of my nipples, and Alex sucks hard. I hiss, and he pushes his cock a bit deeper into my ass, stretching the passageway. Pain flares up but is doused as he returns to gripping my throat, only this time he isn't gentle. His cock enters my ass, and I'm pressing my hands into his shoulders. He releases my breast from between his teeth and puts both hands around my neck.

My ass stretches for him, and he pushes in deeper. Alex's two hands tighten on my neck as he starts to fuck my ass harder.

"Touch yourself," he demands.

I'm a mass of nerve endings and startled with how good he feels in my ass. As he pushes deeper, I drop my hand and touch my swollen clit. I cry out, but the air is minimal as he withdraws slightly from my ass before pushing back in. His movements grow faster, his hands tighten, and my vision blurs, as air isn't accessible to me. My heart thumps wildly as he fucks me with fast and hard strides. His fingers squeeze, and my free hand grabs his forearm like I can stop him, but I don't want to. His hips rise, allowing him to slam into me.

Rubbing my clit has everything smashing through my system, and I'd be calling out if he didn't have his hands around my throat. He fucks my ass frantically, and the room blurs from lack of oxygen as I tilt forward, and every sensation slams with a force I can't stop. I shatter and come as Alex loosens his hands around my throat, but he's still fucking my ass. Each slam is too much, and I fall onto his chest, fighting for air, fighting for control, still riding the wave of my release. Alex slams into me and pauses as he comes in my ass. He withdraws and slams in again, and I can feel his wetness. When he withdraws his cock, his semen slips from my ass.

"Look at me," he demands, breathless.

I do. But it's like an out-of-body experience; my body is still buzzing and confused with how much I just felt at once.

He touches my face and brings me close to him. Pressing his lips against mine, he smiles into the kiss. Sweat gleams on his chest and face.

"I could get used to that." His breath mingles with mine, and I'm staring into his eyes.

His hand leaves my face and runs along my neck. "Did I hurt you?"

I'm shaking my head; my body is trembling from so many feelings. I swallow my throat dry. "No. Not at all."

He smiles before kissing me again. My heart swells and words swim in my head.

I love you.

I've always loved Alex, and I know him, but getting to experience him in this way has me knowing that no one else will ever be able to fulfill me like he can.

He's ruined me for anyone else. As I look at him, I wonder if that's his intention. If it is, he has one hundred percent succeeded.

CHAPTER TWENTY-FOUR

ALEX

NADIA REMAINED QUIET FOR the rest of the day and didn't discuss her mother at all. After leaving her with Blue, I give the hospital a ring. I promised Nadia I would make sure her mother was getting the best care, and I will live up to that promise. She's getting stronger, so having a kidney transplant will be possible. They just want to give her more time. Some of the best doctors are observing her. She won't have the surgery done by the wedding, but I hope it won't be long after.

A meeting with Dillon O'Rourke has me showering and getting dressed in a fresh suit. I check my watch. I need to leave now to meet him. Security has been doubled around the house and no one, not even the Gardaí, is allowed in. I've given my men the go-ahead to use whatever manpower is necessary to keep them at the gates until I return. I don't want to come back to any more surprises. I've also left strict instructions that Nadia isn't allowed to leave. Not even to visit her mother. She's to be kept in the house and watched at all times.

The meeting with Dillon is at the Newgrange Hotel. The same hotel where I met Jack O'Reagan. Because I own it, I know we'll have complete privacy and discretion there.

When I arrive, I find out Dillon hasn't shown yet, so I take care of some business. A new wing is being built out back, and they need me to sign off on some upgrades we hadn't anticipated. The old piping was rotten in areas and needed to be completely replaced. As long as we don't have to close for business, I'm happy to sign off on the new construction.

"Mr. Murphy." The hotel manager, Lucy, gets my attention. "Mr. O'Rourke has arrived and is seated in the bar."

"Thank you." I hand the paperwork back to the builder. "I need this done as soon as possible," I inform him.

He nods. "We have taken on extra men to complete the project."

"Good. Direct any questions to Lucy, and she can inform me."

Lucy smiles.

"How is business?" I ask Lucy as I walk to the bar.

"Booming. All the rooms are filled, and we have a wedding this weekend."

Weddings are where the real money is.

"Thank you, Lucy." I veer off into the bar. A lone barman stands behind the counter, and once I enter, he kicks into action, preparing our drinks.

Dillon is sitting down when I arrive and stands to take my hand. "Alexander."

"Dillon." I take his hand, and his grip is strong. When his hand leaves mine, I open my suit jacket and sit down across from him.

The waiter arrives with two brandies and departs, leaving the room completely. He closes the double doors, giving Dillon and me privacy.

"This is my first visit to one of your hotels." Dillon glances around. "I must say, I'm very impressed."

I don't give a fuck if he's impressed.

"Hmm." I pick up the brandy and take a drink.

Dillon watches me as he sinks back into the leather chair. "How is business?" he asks.

"Booming." I repeat Lucy's earlier words.

"Why am I here?" Dillon sits forward in the chair.

"My hotels may be booming, but other ends of my business aren't," I answer and place the glass of brandy onto the table. I twirl it once before resting my fingers on the rim of the glass.

"I heard about the shipments. The same has been happening to us, Alexander. We did discuss this at our last meeting. So, I ask once again, why am I here? I hope it's to discuss my daughter."

"Our shipments were handed over to the Gardaí, but yours weren't. So that makes me suspicious. And as far as your daughter goes, I'm getting married next week to someone else."

He nods and picks up his glass of brandy. "I heard, and congratulations." He takes a swallow.

I remove my fingers from my glass. "Why ask about your daughter if you already knew?"

He smiles. "You have more siblings. I believe that William will be next to take power, if you fail."

I grin. "I won't fail. But yes, he is next in line."

"Maybe he would consider a joining of families."

Dillon places his glass onto the table and sits fully back in the chair. His face grows serious. "I had nothing to do with your shipment ending up in the Gardaí's hands. We don't behave in such a manner. If your father were alive, he would tell you the same."

"Maybe so. But I had to ask."

Dillon doesn't look impressed. "Then ask me directly, Alexander. If I'm going to be accused, I'd like it put into a full sentence."

He was flexing his own power, and I would give in to his request.

"Did you give the Gardaí our shipments so you could take the West from us?"

"No, I did not."

Do I believe him? It's hard to know. We are all such good fucking liars.

"I had this employee once. He was loyal. A good man. He had run into some circumstances that sent him to me for help." Dillon picks up his drink, but he doesn't bring it to his lips, just holds it on the arm of the chair. "He needed money; his daughter had leukemia. She was only three. So, as he was a good employee and I, a good employer, I gave him the money." He takes a drink.

"That was very kind of you," I state.

"Hmm. His daughter recovered and all was well." He holds up a finger. "But, not long later, he came to me again. His mother had fallen ill, and once again, he needed money. I gave it to him, but she was beyond saving and she died." Dillon moves forward in his seat, his voice lowering.

"The next time he came to me, I didn't allow him to speak. You see, I knew he was coming with another problem. Maybe his dog got run over, or another one of his kids had fallen ill. The true problem wasn't his family. It wasn't even him coming to me with his problems. It was that I was enabling him. What did it say to my men? Come to me with a bruised knee, and I will nurse you?" He smiles. "I shot him dead on the spot." He opens his hands wide. "Problem solved."

"I'm struggling to find the knowledge in your story."

"Sometimes the problem you are trying to solve isn't the problem at all. Maybe the person who is bringing you the problem is the problem."

I take a drink and ponder his words. He knows something, but he isn't saying. Who brought the problem to me about Lexi? Jason had. It was one of his men. Who told Jake about the shipments? That is something I will have to find out.

"I did not touch your shipments, and I won't lie, I am very disappointed you will not marry my daughter. But for your father's sake, I will lay out a final alternative. William will marry her."

We all had to do things for the greater good. I nod. "I will talk to him."

Dillon empties his glass. "I hope he agrees, and we can continue to work together." Dillon stands and buttons his suit jacket. He walks to me and places his hand on my shoulder. "Don't take long getting back to me, Alexander."

He steps away, and I finish my drink. *Maybe the person who is bringing you the problem is the problem.* Dillon's words stay with me as I leave the hotel. Hadn't Aidan said he thinks he found something on Jason? But how would Jason be the problem?

I arrive home to find Jake waiting for me. He's exactly who I'm looking for. He doesn't speak as I unlock my study door, but he follows me in.

"I had a very interesting talk with Dillon O'Rourke."

Jake raises both brows. "Interesting. As in he's the person responsible for the shipments being handed over?"

I sit down behind my desk. "No, I don't think he is. But he wants William to marry his daughter."

Jake grins. "How did William take the news?"

"I haven't told him yet. I've just gotten back. I wanted to ask. Who told you about the shipments being left on the streets?"

Jake sinks into the chair across from me. "Edmond. Why?"

"It's nothing. So what have you got for me?" I ask, knowing I'd have to talk to Edmond about who told him.

"Detective Roberts has been calling. I told him I'd pass on the message that he wants to speak to you."

He can wait.

"So, I have news on the guy who tried to kill Nadia. I gave his mother a visit and surprise, surprise, she's Russian." Jake grins. "Russian and very talkative. Being kept in the nursing home has loosened her old lips. I told her I was a close friend of her son's. She informed me that he's a good boy, not like his father, who worked for the Russian mob." Jake's grin breaks into a smile. "Motherfucker must have been working for the Russians. That's not a coincidence."

I nod. "You're right, and the Russians were at Lexi's. Good work."

"I'll keep digging. Find out what I can at some of the local bars. He could have been low key for them. We will find out who sent him." Jake stands.

"Can you tell Edmond I want him?"

Jake taps the desk before walking away. "I can, no problem."

Once Jake leaves, I sit back in the seat. My mind is spinning. I feel confident ruling out Dillon O'Rourke, but his hands aren't clean either. He knows something he isn't telling me directly. I wonder if Reilan would be more willing to talk.

The door opens and Edmond walks in. "You called, boss?" He walks to the chair.

"This won't take long."

He stays standing.

"Who told you about the shipment of ours being left on the street for the Gardaí?"

Edmond rubs his jaw. "Greg. He got a tip."

"Who is Greg?" I've never heard that name before.

"He is one of Jason's men. He's the one who tipped you off about Lexi's club, too."

He's one of Jason's men. All roads lead back to Jason, but that doesn't add up. My stomach clenches. Jason is the negotiator for the Russians. But he wouldn't betray us.

Or would he?

CHAPTER TWENTY-FIVE

ALEX

"I NEED A FAVOR." Nadia won't look at me. My arm tightens around her. She's naked under the sheets and nestled into my side. The last few days, I haven't made much of a dent in the mystery to our shipments, and neither have the O'Reagans. Jason has been out of town, so I haven't gotten to question him either. The more I think about Jason being involved in the missing shipments, the more unlikely it seems. Had Dillon O'Rourke planted that seed of doubt so I'd go off on a wild goose chase? Between the wedding and having appointments with organizers, I haven't had much time anyway.

"Name it," I say, pressing a kiss to her forehead. She glances up at me, worry swimming in her gaze. "I haven't told my mother about the wedding, and I was hoping you would come with me today."

Today? It's my bachelor party with my brothers. Jason is arriving back in town for it, and I'm hoping to use the night to find out what I can.

"Why haven't you told her?" I thought her mother already knew.

Nadia chews on her lip. "I just haven't found the right time."

The worry has her tightening her hold on the blanket.

"Of course I'll come," I say.

Her gaze widens and she loosens her fingers on the quilt. "Thank you."

I kiss her forehead again. "But I won't be able to stay long." I unravel her from me and get out of the bed. "I have my bachelor party today."

She sits up, keeping the blankets tightened around her body. She watches me as I walk across the room naked, and her gaze trails down to my growing cock. Being around Nadia has that effect on me. No matter how much I have of her, I always want more.

"That's okay."

I open the wardrobe and take out a clean suit and shirt. Laying them on the bed, I look at Nadia. "You should do something with Sally."

She's shaking her head. "I'm not into that. A bachelorette party sounds like my worst nightmare."

I'm not looking forward to my bachelor party either, but my brothers won't have it any other way. "You could go anywhere," I offer, taking the shirt off the hanger and slipping it on.

"We have the honeymoon." Nadia tries to hide a smile.

We're going to Spain. It's on her bucket list. A list I need to get my hands on so I can tick each item off. I pull on fresh boxers and get dressed into my suit.

"Four full days in Spain will be nice." I glance at her and feel an overwhelming amount of gratitude that I finally have what I truly want.

I reach across the bed and take her hand, pressing a soft kiss to her fingers. She's still wearing my ring, and that's all she wore last night as I had my wicked way with her.

"You better get dressed before I change my mind and climb back in." I grin.

Her cheeks fill with color, and she slips from the bed naked. I sit and take her in. She's perfect. Everything about Nadia is perfect. I'm a lucky man. "Does your mother know we're engaged?"

Nadia slides on her underpants. Without looking at me, she answers, "No. She doesn't even know we're together."

I scoff. "This should be interesting."

Nadia glances at me. "I know I should have said something, but the timing never seemed right."

I get off the bed and walk to her as she puts her bra on. "All will be rectified soon."

She doesn't seem convinced. "Your mother will be happy." I press a soft kiss to her lips.

She nods, forcing a smile, but she doesn't speak. I let her finish getting dressed.

"We can have breakfast after." She's very nervous, and I didn't expect that.

I don't like her going out with an empty stomach, but I agree. She wants to get this done and over with.

***

The hospital is quiet, and Nadia hasn't spoken a word since we left the house. "Do you want me to do all the talking?"

She's playing with the ring on her finger, and when the elevator doors open, she doesn't step out.

"Nadia?"

She looks up at me. "We need to make her believe this."

I frown and the doors close behind us. "This is real. We are getting married." I walk to her and take her face in my hands. "When she sees us together, she will know it's real."

Some of the worry is erased from Nadia's face. "It's just so much to land at her feet two days before the wedding. I should have told her sooner." She starts to fret.

I tighten my hold on her face. "Listen to me. Your mother will be happy. Just wait and see." I give her a kiss and take her hand in mine. I press the elevator button and the doors open. Nadia is still looking terrified as I lead her down the hallway and stop at her mother's hospital room. I give her hand a small squeeze before I enter.

Her mother is sitting up, and she looks so much better than she did before she was moved into private care.

"Alex." She smiles wide and her smile widens even further as she notices Nadia behind me. Her gaze dips to our joined hands, and she's looking back at her daughter.

"You look marvelous," I say, releasing Nadia's hand and walking to my future mother-in-law. I place a kiss on her cheek.

"Very charming, Alexander. But I do feel so much better." When I look in her eyes, I see the gratitude. "Thanks to you."

I wave off her thanks. "My father wouldn't have had it any other way."

She smiles fondly. "He was a good man."

I don't respond. Was he a good man? To her, yes. To others, yes. But to me? Not so much.

I sit down and let Nadia pass to greet her mother.

"This is such a lovely surprise. I wasn't expecting you." Her gaze dips to the ring again.

"We have something to share."

She nods. "I see that." She's back to looking at Nadia, who isn't sitting. She looks stiff and terrified. My God. She's making this harder. I stand and place a hand on Nadia's shoulder. She looks up at me, and I take the moment to really look at the women I love. I lean in and press a kiss to her lips.

"We are engaged," I say, still looking into Nadia's eyes before I glance back at her mother.

She isn't doing cartwheels, but she isn't appalled either. "You're dating?"

"I wanted to tell you, but it never seemed like the right time." Nadia clears her throat, but she reaches for my hand and takes it. "I'm happy, Mam. I really am."

Nadia does sound happy, and her mother must hear it, too. Her gaze grows watery. "If you are happy, so am I. That's all that matters."

"I'll take care of her," I say.

She nods at me. "How long has this been going on?"

Nadia looks uncomfortable again. This isn't hard for me. "When she was ten, I kissed her and knew I would marry her one day."

Nadia's head snaps toward me, her gaze widening in surprise.

"I've been obsessed with your daughter ever since."

My confession catches both women by surprise, but Nadia's mother smiles. "Give your mother a hug."

Nadia exhales and steps into her mother's embrace. "Have you set a date?" her mother asks when some of the shock passes.

"The wedding is in two days," I say, knowing Nadia will stumble across this final block. Better to rip off the Band-Aid. "My people will make sure you are there."

"I have nothing to wear." Her hand covers her mouth. "Two days."

"My people will sort everything out—your clothes, a car. The doctors will be there with you."

Tears spill from her eyes. "I don't know what to say."

I smile. "Say you are happy for us. That's all Nadia is worried about." I take my soon-to-be wife's hand again and bring it to my lips.

"I'm happy. I'm so happy," she cries.

Nadia lets my hand go and sits on the bed beside her mother. "I should have told you sooner."

Her mother shakes her head, wiping her tears away. "We all withhold things thinking it isn't the right time."

Something passes between the women before they embrace.

I sit down and ignore the buzzing of my phone. No doubt Aidan is at my house waiting for me, but I stay as Nadia's mother lets the news really sink in. The excitement between the women bubbles, and I soak in the joy.

After an hour and several missed calls, I nudge Nadia. "We need to go."

She nods. "I'll be back tomorrow." Nadia kisses her mother.

And I give her one final promise to take care of her daughter. We leave with a happier Nadia, and I know keeping my brothers waiting was worth it.

***

"What the fuck, Alex?" Aidan says after Nadia goes into the house.

"I had something to do," I answer so he doesn't start.

But he seems happy I'm here. He walks to his car. "Let's go."

I get in and see Matty and William in the back. "Where is Jason?"

"He's meeting us there," William says. I still haven't told him about his upcoming marriage to Dillon O'Rourke's daughter. I'd let the drinks start to flow before I dropped that bomb on him.

"How are you, Matty?" I ask as I buckle up.

Matty salutes me as I turn to him. "Ready to get this party started." He grins, and it's nice to see him without a phone in his hands.

We leave, and I feel content knowing that Nadia is happy inside, where she will remain until I get back.

"So, are you going to tell me where we're going?" I ask Aidan. He's the driver, and so far, they have been tight lipped about the outing.

"To a strip club, of course," William says from the back seat.

"Delightful," I deadpan.

William laughs. "Well, I'm looking forward to it."

"You better behave yourself. You may soon be following down the same path as I am," I say. There's no point holding back. He's in the car with nowhere to go, so telling him now seems as good a time as ever, I decide.

"What the fuck are you talking about?" William grips the back of my seat, pulling himself closer.

"Yeah, what are you talking about?" Aidan asks, giving me a curious glance.

"I had a meeting with Dillon O'Rourke."

William curses. "You made a deal."

"It's for the greater good," I say.

"He wants to give his daughter's hand to William," I inform Aidan, who's waiting on my answer.

I turn so I can see William's face.

"What does she look like?" he asks, seeming unbothered.

"I've never seen her."

William shakes his head. "If she's ugly, that's a deal breaker."

I grin. "So, you *will* marry her."

He shrugs. "I've done worse for our family. Marrying should be easy."

Yeah, he's right. We all know we might end up in an arranged marriage, and considering all the shit we do for our family, it's nearly the easiest part.

"So I can tell him yes?" I sit forward.

William exhales loudly. "You could have waited until I had my fun to tell me."

"I know I could have," I say.

"Congratulations," Aidan teases.

"Will I be your best man?" Matty asks William.

"You're dead fucking right you will be, because you will be next, Matty. Everyone else is taken."

Matty doesn't answer, and I know if this were his arrangement, he would say no. Matty wouldn't be as quick to jump into bed with a strange woman. So I'm grateful he wasn't selected by Dillon O'Rourke.

Aidan slows down the vehicle, and we drive into an airline hangar.

"Are we going abroad?" I ask, hoping we aren't. I don't want to be far from Nadia.

"Nope," Aidan answers as he drives toward a hangar that has a plane inside. The plane's door is open, a red carpet leading up to the steps.

"This is the party." Aidan stops the car, and William and Matty get out. I follow suit and march behind my brothers across the red carpet. Each of us is handed a glass of champagne, and we board the plane.

Music pulses from inside the plane, and as we board, Jason stands up holding a half-empty glass of wine. He smiles at us. "I thought you would never arrive."

I walk toward him. He's seated at the bar, where the bartender is mixing several cocktails.

"Was this your idea?" I ask, clinking my glass with his.

"No, it was Matty's," Jason admits.

Matty, William, and Aidan sit down on the couches.

"I was thinking of a party bus, but I thought a party plane would be more fun." Matty winks.

The plane is definitely different. I sit down beside my brothers, and Jason joins us.

"So, where have you been?" I ask the million-dollar question.

And what exactly have you been up to?

CHAPTER TWENTY-SIX

ALEX

"No. No. This is a no-business zone." Aidan leans forward, hitting his glass off each of ours. "No business. Just fun."

I'd have my chance to ask my questions. Aidan glares at me, and I can tell he knows something. I want to know too, but we have time. We drink and reminisce. I'm surprised with how much my brothers remember about Nadia and how she always got me into trouble. I hadn't thought they noticed. But clearly, they had.

"Father was so fucking mad that day." William is laughing. I'm not happy he has a drink in his hand. He's been sober, but because of the occasion, I don't remark.

Matty gets up and goes to the bar.

"I doubt it was anything like my old man," Jason says, the drink showing in his gaze. His father tortured him. We hadn't known until recently what Frank had inflicted on him.

"No. Father never raised his hand to us. You know that," I respond dryly to Jason.

"Sometimes a slap is easier," Aidan chimes in, and the atmosphere grows tense.

"I highly doubt that. Having your skin burnt is fucking torture. I can deal with a few words."

I don't respond but sit back and watch Jason unravel under the influence of drink.

"You guys need to chill the fuck out." Matty returns with a bottle of Budweiser swinging from his fingers. "This is meant to be a party, not a dick measuring contest."

"Speaking of parties." William grins and gets up. "Here comes the entertainment."

We all look to the door as three women, all with platinum hair, enter. The pink silk gowns are shed as they walk toward us. The white undergarments are complimented with white suspenders and red heels. I'm picturing Nadia dressed like that, and my cock comes alive.

"Which one of you is the groom?" the lead girl says with a smile on her face. The red lipstick stretches her white smile.

"I am," William says and taps his legs. "Well, I will be soon."

"You're getting married?" Jason's mood has plummeted as he takes another drink.

"Yep. To Dillon O'Rourke's daughter." William speaks while looking at the woman who approaches him.

One of the other women changes the music to something sultry, and William takes the lap dance I have no desire for.

One of the clones approaches Matty, but he declines. His face is a mask of stone. No one would want to be in his company; he may as well have a fuck-off sign on his forehead.

She quickly moves onto Jason, who flicks two fingers at her. "Move on," he tells her.

She turns to me and I grin. "I am the groom."

"Isn't this my lucky day?" she declares, walking to me. She turns and slowly descends onto my lap, grinding her ass onto my hard cock.

"I see you're as excited as I am." I grip her hips, and she turns her head and smiles down at me.

"I'm thinking of my wife-to-be," I admit.

She chuckles. "Sure, you are."

"If you don't want her, I'll take her." William calls her over, and I'm happy to let her go. The third girl approached Aidan, but he also declines.

"Who organized the entertainment?" I ask.

Aidan points his glass at Matty.

I'm surprised because he looks like he'd rather be anywhere else but here.

"It's mandatory for a bachelor party, or so William told me," Matty says dryly.

That makes me laugh as William enjoys all the women. When they start to strip, he rises. "Why don't you show me all your skills back here." They giggle and follow William to the back of the plane.

Once the room clears, I focus on Jason, who's seething. What the fuck is wrong with him?

"I need to have a word with your informant," I say.

"No business," Aidan declares as he sits beside Jason, tightening our circle.

"Which one?" Jason asks. Sitting forward, he places his glass onto the table.

"The one who told you about Lexi. The same one who informed my men about the Gardaí having our shipment. Greg, I think it is."

Jason doesn't blink but finally nods. "No problem. I can arrange a meeting. Do you want to tell me what this is about?"

Aidan gives up telling us not to talk about business and gets himself another drink.

"Just a hunch," I say.

"A fucking hunch about what?" Jason's aggression isn't welcomed.

I grin. "About where his loyalties lie."

Jason sits back. "His loyalties lie with me."

We will see.

"Will you arrange the meeting?"

Aidan returns with a fresh drink for us all.

"No problem." Jason takes the drink, and the noise from the back of the plane has Matty turning up the music.

"To a very lucky man." Aidan holds up his glass to me, and everyone follows suit. The conversation veers away from Jason, and we talk about our childhood, some of the more pleasant times.

***

I wake on the plane with the mother of all hangovers. Opening one eye, I sit up and push the blonde girl off my knee. The three strippers are still here. White powder on the table tells me the party went long into the night.

Fuck's sake. William was meant to be clean. I run both my hands down my face. Aidan raises his cup of coffee at me.

"Good morning, sunshine." He grins.

I grumble and look around. I do a double take at William, who's asleep on the floor wrapped in one of the stripper's pink nightgowns.

Aidan laughs. "He can't control himself."

"Clearly." Jesus, I hope he learns to quit if he's going to marry Dillon O'Rourke's daughter.

Matty is curled up on the chair beside us. I nudge him and he wakes up. "How's the head?" I ask.

Mine is fucking pounding.

"Not bad." Matty gets up and stretches.

I'm looking around the plane for Jason, but he isn't here. "Where is Jason?"

Aidan answers. "I woke up about an hour ago, and he wasn't here."

Aidan looks fresh, and his coffee looks good. "Do you want one?" he asks as I eye the cup.

I nod.

"Ah, what the fuck." William starts to rise. The silk gown slips open at the front, and we're all greeted with his morning wood.

"Fuck's sake, William," Matty barks.

William stretches, hiding nothing. When he looks down, he gives an unapologetic smirk. As he tries to close the nightgown, the material won't budge.

"You look fucking ridiculous," Matty declares, getting up and slipping on his jacket. "I've got to get to the office. I have a meeting with our tax consultant."

I can't function right now. I wave at him with two fingers as I accept the coffee from Aidan.

"See you tomorrow at the church." Matty pats my shoulder as he passes.

"Yeah, don't be late," I mumble while taking a sip of the coffee.

William pops open a bottle of Budweiser.

"Do you think that's wise?" Aidan asks.

"It's the cure. So, it's wise." William drinks half the bottle down in one gulp, and I exchange a gaze with Aidan.

"Can you put some clothes on?" I say.

William finishes the bottle. "Yeah, I don't know where they are."

One of the blondes starts to wake up, rubs her eyes, and when she sees William, she smiles.

"Do you want to help me find my clothes?" He winks at her.

She's on her feet like a newborn deer and following William to the back of the plane.

"That's my cue to leave," I say to Aidan.

"Mine, too." Aidan places the cup onto the table, and we leave together. Outside, the sun is too bright.

"Can you drive?" I walk around to the passenger seat without waiting for his answer.

When I get into his car, I pop the glove compartment and take out some pain pills. I swallow a few of them as we leave the hangar.

"Did you have a good night?" Aidan sounds refreshed.

"Yes, but why aren't you dying?"

"I stopped drinking when Jason started talking about his past. Someone needed to be sober."

"He's a mess," I say.

"Something is eating away at him," Aidan responds.

I glance at Aidan. "You sound like you found something on him. What is it?"

"Honestly, I'm not sure if it's anything." Aidan sounds distant.

"Tell me and I'll decide."

Aidan exhales. "He's been having meetings with Kira's uncle."

I glance at Aidan. "That's not odd. He's part of the Russian mob."

"Yeah, but Jason doesn't answer to him. He's a brigadier for the Russian mob, Alex. He doesn't go through Jason, or should I say Jason doesn't go through him. I think they're doing something on the side."

I dig my palms into my eyes, my brain not working fully. "Like what?"

"I can't figure that out right now."

I lie back. Aidan can figure that one out. I don't think it's anything to worry about. The Russian mob has a different hierarchy than we do. Who the fuck knows how it all works.

Aidan drops me off at the house. "I'll see you in the morning," he says.

I'm ready for bed. When I get in, Jake is there. "I don't have the head for bad news."

"Nice to have been invited." He doesn't sound offended at all.

"Matty organized it," I say.

"I'm sure it was riveting, then." He laughs.

Matty is known to be the quiet, dry one among us all, but I think he's the dark horse of us brothers. It's always the quiet ones you have to watch out for.

"We had the party on a plane, and we even had strippers," I tell Jake as I walk to the stairs.

"Not bad at all. Edmond took Nadia to see her mother."

Nadia. Her name makes my body relax. "Okay, I'm going to get some sleep. I don't want to be disturbed. Nadia, of course, can disturb me." I say as I clear the steps. Jake's soft laughter follows me up the stairs.

I'd love my wife to be beside me now. Maybe sleep first, and when she gets back, I can enjoy her delicious body.

***

It's the morning of the wedding. I can't believe it's here. I had to vacate the house. Sally is with Nadia. I wanted to stay, but they didn't want me to see her before the wedding. We couldn't even spend last night together, and I slept most of the day away.

"How are you holding up?" Aidan asks. He pats me on the back, and I sit down on one of the pews. The church is full, and my nerves are getting the better of me. Jesus, I didn't think anything could make me nervous.

"It's close to showtime." Matty enters. He's a groomsman, along with Aidan. He looks very smart.

I get to my feet and fix my jacket.

"William is out front scanning the crowd for Dillon O'Rourke so he can see if his future wife is ugly." Matty grins. "I worry about him."

"We all do," Aidan says, and his tone is more serious.

"But today is about Alex." Aidan stops in front of me. "Are you ready?"

I nod. "Yes. Let's go."

We leave the small room that's directly across from the altar. The bells of the church ring, and the crowd settles down.

I'm tempted to fix my jacket again but keep still. A Mafia man doesn't fidget. Jesus Christ, I'm so nervous. The bells chime again, and I'm looking at the doors like everyone else, waiting for that moment for Nadia to enter. I know she will look like a vision. I'm waiting and waiting.

I glance at Aidan, who gives me a reassuring nod. I don't look out into the crowd. Every Mafia leader is here to witness this union. I don't want to focus on their faces. The only one I want to see is Nadia's.

That's the only face I don't see. As time drags on and the crowd starts to whisper, my nerves turn to panic. Something has happened.

Something has happened to Nadia.

"Give me your phone," I say to Matty, knowing he wouldn't go anywhere without his device.

He takes it out of his pocket, and I ring Nadia's phone. Dread floods my system. I end the call and turn my back on the crowd. I ring Jake, and when his phone rings out, I know something has happened.

CHAPTER TWENTY-SEVEN

NADIA

"You need to calm down, Nadia." Sally tries to comfort me. "You'll ruin your makeup."

A bang on the bedroom door silences both of us.

"Open the door," Jake barks again.

This is a mess.

"Go away, Jake," Sally shouts back.

I'm staring at myself in the full-length mirror. I know I can't go through with the wedding. The guilt of my mother's lies weighs too heavily on my shoulders.

"Tell me what's wrong," Sally begs for the tenth time.

How can I tell her all of this is built on lies? Lies that my mother spun.

"I just can't marry him," I whisper and that brings a fresh wave of tears. I love him, but I can't walk down the aisle knowing that Alex wouldn't be marrying me if my mother had told the truth. None of this would be happening. I should have been honest with him.

"I'll break down the door if you don't open it!" Jake roars.

I turn from the mirror and march across the room.

"Nadia," Sally pleads.

I unlock the door, and Jake nearly tumbles in but rights himself. "What is going on?" he barks at me.

"We just need a few more minutes," Sally interjects.

Minutes won't fix this. Nothing will.

"Nadia, Alex is ringing," Jake says. "What do I say to him?"

My stomach tightens. Jesus, he must be so angry.

"I don't know," I say honestly. What should I say to him? I know talking about this at the altar isn't the right place.

Jake's phone starts to ring again. "I have to tell him something."

"Tell him I'm not coming." My throat closes and I choke up.

Jake nods and turns his back on me, taking the call. "She's fine. I've been trying to talk to her. She locked herself in her room." Jake's voice grows distant as he walks away.

"You don't have to marry him if you don't want to," Sally says softly.

"I want to marry him, just…" Not under the circumstances.

I love him. I love him so much, but I can't start our life on a lie.

Pounding footsteps on the stairs sends my heart into an erratic beat. I want to lock the door and lock out the world, but I can't move as Alex storms into the room. I've never seen anyone look so… devastated. He's breathless and stops when he sees me. His gaze drags across my entire dress and stops at my face. "I thought something happened to you," he whispers.

"I'm sorry." I swallow the tears. "I'm so sorry."

He walks to me but stops while shaking his head. "Why?" He sounds bewildered.

Sally is still in the room with us, and when I look at her, she blinks a few times. "I'll give you some space."

I nod and wait until she leaves.

"I can't marry you," I say. Something inside me cracks at the vulnerable look in Alex's gaze. "There was no burglary." The words tumble from my mouth as tears spill from my eyes. "I know if my mother hadn't lied, you wouldn't have brought me to your home and seen me as an option to marry you. You would have entered the arranged marriage, and I would have continued to be your PA." My words hurt so much, but they're the truth. "I'm so sorry I didn't tell you. She made the burglary up so I wouldn't worry about her health."

He hasn't moved, and the vulnerable look that was there only seconds ago slowly starts to lift.

"I was so afraid that if I did tell you, you would call off the wedding." I knot my hands together. It's all out on the table, and the fear of God is in me. Will he nod and say I'm right, that he would have called the wedding off?

He continues to stare at me.

"So, I've done you a favor. You can marry that other girl." I inhale a shaky breath. I've lost him. I've lost him, and it's my own fault. I'm ready to plead with him, to ask for another chance, when he walks to me.

"You should have told me." His eyes roam my face. "Fuck's sake, Nadia, you should have just said."

I blink and tears spill. "I was afraid," I admit.

"You should have told me. It wouldn't have mattered to me."

Shivers break out across my flesh. "What?"

He grabs my face. "I would have married you no matter what." His words are growled.

"I couldn't start this marriage off with such a lie."

He releases my face and turns away from me.

"Alex," I say softly.

"You didn't have to stand me up at the altar." When he looks at me, it's a mixture of relief and anger. "I wouldn't have cared."

"I care. I don't like lies. I should have told you."

He nods. "You should have. But not like this." He opens his arms wide.

"I'm sorry," I repeat, as I can't think of what else to say. "I only just found out. She had lied to me, too."

He frowns. "I don't give a fuck about the burglary." He sighs.

More tears pour down my cheeks, and he's back to holding my face. "I thought something happened to you." His voice is low. "Do you remember when we were kids, and we stayed up all night watching TV? You ate so many sweets you were sick the next day."

I swallow my tears and nod. "Yeah, you had gotten me so many dip dabs."

His laugh causes his breath to brush across my face. "You couldn't resist the dip dabs."

He presses his lips to mine. When he looks into my eyes, I can almost see the memory. "My father had found out we stayed up late. I was tired at my studies, and he wasn't happy. And when you didn't arrive with your mother, I thought he did something to you. I carried that fear all day."

His hands tighten on my face. "It wasn't until the next day I found out you had just been sick, but for a moment, I'd thought the worst." He presses his lips against mine. "That's what this felt like, that fear of thinking I've lost the most important person to me."

I want to say I'm sorry again, but he hasn't finished talking.

"Only this time, it wouldn't be my father's doing but my own." He releases my face. "We all have secrets, Nadia."

Sadness floods his gaze.

"I didn't know your father was like that, Alex." He always seemed so lovely to me. I never knew the depths of his disapproval of my and Alex's relationship.

"My father was a wanker," Alex says.

His anger makes me flinch.

"Anyone who stood in his way didn't stand a chance." Alex walks away again. His hands tighten into fists.

I take a few paces until I can reach out and touch his tense shoulder. "Alex." I don't know what his father did to him, but this is so much deeper than I could have ever imagined.

"He wanted me to kill Jason."

The air is sucked out of the room.

I learned recently that Jason isn't their brother but a cousin. None of the boys spoke of it, but it was gossip among the staff.

"Why?" I ask.

Alex faces me. "So his fortune would return to me. He lost nearly all of it to his brother, Frank. If I didn't kill Jason, someone else would. So…"

I drag air into my lungs as Alex glares at me. He's breathing heavily, and I fear if I move as much as an inch, he will stop.

"I killed my father so he couldn't hurt Jason."

My legs wobble, and I'm waiting for Alex to laugh, but he doesn't. He stares at me.

I'm shaking my head. Has he lost his mind?

"Your father took his life." Is that knowledge so heavy on Alex that he has made up this twisted fantasy? "That wasn't your fault, Alex."

I reach for him, but he steps away with a sinister smirk on his face.

"I made it look that way."

Bile rises up my throat. "You made it look like your father took his life?" I whisper.

The full impact of what he's saying drives me a few steps away from him.

"It was him or Jason. I told you before that it's kill or be killed. I couldn't accept Jason dying."

I'm shaking my head. He killed his father. "What about Jason?"

"What about him?" Alex asks.

"Does he know what you did for him?"

Alex's anger falls away like a second skin. "No. No one does."

I close my eyes. Oh, God.

My eyelids snap open as his hands touch my shoulders.

"I did what was necessary." His words brush across my face, his gaze pleading with me to understand. "We all have our secrets. Now you have mine, Nadia."

My legs can't hold me up any longer, and I walk easily out of Alex's embrace and slump down on the bed. He doesn't move from where he stands.

"I hate your world," I say to my hands.

His footsteps approach before his shoes appear in front of me. The bed dips, and Alex's large hand encases mine. "Me, too."

I look at him, and I realize I don't fear him. I should, especially after his confession, but I pity the world he's forced to live in. "When does it stop?"

His Adam's apple bobbles. "I don't know."

"How can we bring kids into this world?" I plead.

He smiles, which confuses me. "You want to have kids with me?"

I let it all flutter away and just give into this precise moment with Alex. "I love you, Alex. I always have." I reach up and touch his face. His eyelids close, cutting me off from his pain.

"But I won't bring children into this world who will grow up and have to decide whether they kill you, or..." He looks at me.

"Or each other." I can't bear that kind of pain.

"I can't bring kids into this world wondering when the Gardaí will drag them from their beds." My lip wobbles, and I fight with my emotions to say what I want to say. "I won't go to sleep in a hotel room and worry if I'll be shot or if one of my kids will."

Tears fall freely. "I can't bear that kind of loss. I'm not cut out for this life."

The truth is more painful than I could have ever imagined, and I see that pain reflected in Alex's gaze. For a second, I think he might cry.

That would undo me.

"What are you saying?" He touches my face, his fingers moving across the flesh like he's trying to memorize what I look like.

"I thought I didn't want to go forward with the wedding because of the lie about my mother, but I realize that it's not about that, or you. It's about the future. I can't do this."

I sniffle as my throat and eyes burn. "I can't see a future like this." I close my eyes, and my mouth fills with salty tears. "I love you. I love you so much."

I look up into Alex's face. "That's why I have to leave."

I press a kiss to his lips, and I know I need to walk away. I need to release his face, but my fingers won't loosen. I'm so weak. "I love you," I cry into the kiss before I find some inner strength and break free.

"Is this because of what I did to my father?" Alex asks.

It should be. I shake my head. "No, Alex. It's refusing to have one of my kids sit here and confess some horrible crime they were forced to do to someone they loved. I can't do this."

I stand up and each step is painful, but I know I can't ask Alex to leave his position. I can't live like this either.

"Where do you think you're going?" Alex asks.

I turn and he's standing. He no longer looks ready to cry.

I shrug. "Home. There is no threat there."

He shakes his head. "That's not an option, Nadia."

I'm ready to fight back, but I'm exhausted. He knows what I'm saying is right, though.

"You aren't leaving me," he says, taking a step closer.

"Ever."

CHAPTER TWENTY-EIGHT

ALEX

I'M FIGHTING A LOSING battle. I think I've always known that, but watching Nadia try to leave the bedroom reinforces the truth.

"Alex, I'm sorry. I can't do this."

She's a picture in her wedding dress, with tears staining her cheeks. Those stains go so deep, right down into her soul. Her chin wobbles as she tightens her eyelids. "I just can't."

I get up off the bed and walk to her. "You can't leave."

I won't allow it.

Her lids snap open, and frustration and hurt have her brows knitted together before she can tell me all the reasons she can't be with me. I close the distance between us and take her hands.

"I love you," I confess.

Her chest rises and falls rapidly.

"I love you so much that I can't lose you, Nadia. Not today, not tomorrow, not ever."

She blinks and tears fall. "I'm not sure if love is enough."

I nod. "I know. I'll give it up." Saying the words out loud is liberating. This life isn't one I want, either, and hearing Nadia speak of children has me realizing I want so much more than this existence.

"I'll step down." I'm nodding as I speak. "I'll hand the reins over to William."

She's shaking her head, hope blossoming like a new bud in her gaze. "Can you just do that?"

Her words are breathy.

I lean in and kiss her lips. "I can do whatever I want." I smile into the kiss.

"Will they allow you to leave?" Hope continues to grow, drying up her tears.

"I have no one to answer to but myself. But, yes, my brothers will understand. We all have done the unthinkable for love. We have fought and killed for it, so walking away from this life won't be easy, but they will understand."

She's in my arms before I can blink, sobbing. "We can be together."

Her relief becomes my relief, and I wrap my arms around Nadia. "Forever."

That's what this means. She's mine forever.

My phone rings in my pocket, smashing the moment. I release Nadia and take the device out of my pocket. Aidan's name flashes up on screen. I answer it while touching Nadia's cheek. She leans into my touch.

"Everything is okay. Nadia is safe," I say while looking into her eyes. "Go ahead with the celebrations. We won't be coming."

"What do you want me to tell people?" Aidan sounds bewildered.

"Tell them to have fun. Nadia and I are going on our honeymoon."

Aidan sighs. "Are you sure everything is alright?"

I smile at Nadia before releasing her face. "I promise, brother. I will explain everything later."

"Okay. I'll let them know."

"Thanks, Aidan." I end the call and slip the phone into my pocket.

"Is everyone mad?" Nadia chews on her lip.

"No. I should have never forced you to marry me, Nadia. When you're ready, we can get married." I've made so many bad choices, but now I have a chance to rectify them.

She's smiling, but she seems like a bottle of emotions, the cork ready to pop. "Go get packed. I've one thing to do, and then we can leave." I press a kiss to her forehead.

"Okay." She's relieved.

I open the bedroom door and find Sally sitting on the stairs. The moment she sees me, she rises, worry etched into her face. She's a good friend to wait here for Nadia.

"We're going on our honeymoon. Will you help Nadia pack?"

"Of course, sir." The minute she passes me, she rushes into the room.

I enter my study and sit down behind my desk. I dial Jason's number, and he answers.

"What is happening? Aidan said you were going on your honeymoon?"

I can imagine all the confusion.

"Everything is fine. Nadia isn't ready to marry yet. So, enjoy the day. I wanted to ask about Greg, your informant. Did you manage to organize the meeting? I'd like to have it today, preferably in the next hour before I leave."

Silence drags out.

"Jason?"

"I did organize the meeting, but unfortunately, Greg was shot during a drug run."

And there is a lie. Most likely, Jason had him clipped. So, what is my brother hiding? "That's very unfortunate."

"Indeed," Jason deadpans.

"I'll look into this when I get back."

"No need, brother. We're already tracking down the person responsible."

I'm pretty sure I'm talking to the person responsible.

"Keep me informed." I end the call, and worry gnaws and bites at my flesh. What are you hiding, Jason? What are we all hiding? I have my own secret I never thought I would breathe a word of, but Nadia knows, and she's still here. My brothers wouldn't be as understanding or forgiving. That, I know.

****

The plane touches down in Madrid, Spain. Nadia's excitement is contagious as she tries to look out the plane window. "It's so pretty here."

"That's why I have my second home here," I inform Nadia.

Her gaze widens. "You have another house here," she repeats.

The seat belt light flashes, and she's out of her seat quickly. Her eagerness to get off the plane has me following her closely. A limo waits at the end of the red carpet. I wanted this to be perfect for Nadia.

"I've never left Ireland." She's in awe as she races down the steps. The yellow sundress catches the light, and she's like a flower in the weeds. Breathtaking. All I can think about is taking that dress off her and having my wicked way.

"Congratulations, Mr. and Mrs. Murphy."

I hadn't informed the staff, but I thank them before Nadia starts explaining. I accept the two glasses of champagne. Nadia slides in the back, and I hand her a flute before I get in beside her. The inside of the limo is cool as the air conditioning keeps the stifling Spanish heat at bay.

The limo rolls out of the private landing strip and we travel upward into the red mountains. Nadia sips her champagne and rolls down the window. I've been here a few times, but it's always been on business. Watching Nadia close her eyes and inhale the fresh air makes me see this place differently. Every experience with her feels different. No matter how small the experience, she makes me feel alive.

She glances at me with a delicious smile on her face. "This place is like a picture."

I move closer to her and look out the window at the blue skies that roll into the red mountains. Dust rises as we pass, and the lone bushes show how reclusive this area is.

We slow down as the large golden gates creak open, and we enter the four-story villa I designed.

"Wow." Nadia is half-hanging out the window, the flute of champagne forgotten. When the limo stops, the door is opened, and my butler takes both glasses as we get out.

"You can leave the luggage on the bottom floor," I instruct.

Security is stationed around the premises, reminding me that no matter where I am, there is always a threat. Nadia's shoulders stiffen, and I wonder if she's thinking the same thing. I slip my hand into hers. Her large blue eyes stare up at me.

"When I leave my brothers, all this security won't be necessary." I press a kiss to her shoulder, and she relaxes.

"This is magnificent." The white Villa has four floors. Windows are placed sporadically across the front of the building. The length of them allows an optimal amount of light inside.

The red roof is stark against the white, but it all looks perfect. With the greenery around my home and an abundance of flowers, it's picture perfect. The staff move past us with our luggage.

"Why don't you explore as I speak to Reggie, the head of security here." I release Nadia, and like an excited child, she enters the house after the staff.

Reggie is waiting for me in the outside security hut.

"Great to have you back, boss." He grins. Reggie is in his late fifties, has a military background, and is no stranger to guns. "The men were getting fat and lazy since you left."

I grin. "No fat on you." I tap his tight abs for emphasis.

"I keep up my workout routine." He continues to grin. "How long are you staying for?"

"Five days, but we might return for good soon."

Reggie's grin turns to a smile. "We would be delighted."

I grip his shoulder. "Has there been any trouble in the area?"

He shakes his head. "All quiet. We have had two new families move in at the foot of the mountain. They come from money, the good kind."

I laugh. Not the type that's coated in blood is what he means. So, they aren't criminals. "That's great." Decent people in the area are welcome. I don't want anyone else shitting in my backyard, so we made sure some sales didn't go through. I've only ever had to run off a crime family once. It was messy, but now that I might settle here, it will be worth it.

Nadia will be safer here than in Ireland, and the thought of bringing children into the world makes Spain a prime location.

"Keep up the good work." I leave Reggie and enter the house. The cool air is a nice contrast on my flesh from the heat outside. That's something I would have to get used to.

I have no idea what we would do in Spain. Maybe open a hotel. I have the experience.

I find Nadia standing on the veranda overlooking the back garden. The pool sparkles under the sun, and when I approach, she turns to me.

"I can't get over this place."

I reach Nadia and take her hand in mine. I look out at the mountains that wall in our back garden. "It's safe."

"It's picture perfect." She's staring out into the clear blue sky, and I could watch her all day.

"It is," I say.

She smiles up at me, and when she blushes, I take her face in my hands and kiss her.

"It has great schools," I say.

Her gaze searches my face. "You would live here?"

"*We* would live here."

She's taken aback, and I know I'm throwing a lot at her in one go.

"We can always discuss it." I feel slightly deflated, but I also need her to understand what I'm asking of her.

She shakes her head. "No, this place"—she's looking back out at the pool—"would be perfect, Alex. Just, my mother…"

I bring her hand to my lips and kiss her fingers. I love that she still wears my ring. "Could live with us. She would have great care here, too."

"It's just so much. Everything you're doing for me."

Her emotions sparkle in her eyes.

"I love you, and I'm doing this for me, too." I kiss her lips. "I love you," I repeat, knowing I'd give up the world for her. I will give up my world for her and create a new life here.

"I love you, too," she says.

"The food is ready, sir."

My butler has me breaking away from Nadia. "Thank you."

I lead Nadia down the five steps, where the food is laid out on a large white marble table. It's an extravagant piece of furniture—a piece that was in the original building I had torn down. I salvaged a few unique pieces; this table being one.

The large marble chairs are fixed in place. Red padding makes them comfortable. Once Nadia is seated, I join her. The arched stone railing lets us see the view, yet gives us the feeling of privacy. The red awning overhead casts a shadow across the table, cutting off the light.

Nadia inhales deeply, smiles, and picks up a glass of wine.

"I could get used to this," she declares.

"Good." I clink my glass with hers. Because so could I.

CHAPTER TWENTY-NINE

ALEX

"Take me for a walk." Nadia sits back, sipping wine. She's more relaxed than I've ever seen her. I wipe my face with a napkin and get to my feet while holding out my hand.

Nadia smiles and places her glass onto the table before accepting my outstretched fingers.

We don't have to go back into the house, so I take the twenty steps along the back of the building and into the gardens.

Nadia pauses at the sea-blue pool, our reflection so still in the water.

"Do you want to go for a swim?" I ask, hoping she does. I can imagine her in a bikini.

"Maybe later." She leads this time, and I'm happy to follow her. Her hand is still in mine, and I raise our joined fingers to my mouth, where I press a kiss. We weave our way through the gardens that are in full bloom all year round.

"It's so peaceful." Nadia smiles up at me.

We move onto rough terrain that's informing us we are leaving the manicured gardens and entering more unkempt territory. My mind jumps to enemies behind every rock, and I don't like the feeling of not having my gun on me. I should have packed it. My home has plenty of weapons, and my security would have checked the area, but I can't stop my mind from wandering to the thought of threats.

The red clay under our feet causes dust to rise and quickly coats our shoes. I'm also aware how we leave footprints, and there are no others. I try to relax.

The steep climb has me pausing. "Don't you want to go back?"

Nadia's gaze is full of mischievousness. "I want to explore."

"I can think of other things we can explore."

Her cheeks heat, and I tug her hand, pulling her slightly toward me.

She giggles. "We have time for that."

I press a kiss to her lips. "We have the rest of our lives, but I also like the saying 'Never put off until tomorrow what you can do today.'"

"I don't think that saying applies to this." She's smiling so wide, and I want to kiss her, but Nadia is eager to get to the top. We're close, and I continue the climb with her.

At the hood of the small cliff, we can see other houses embedded into the mountainside. She stands and closes her eyes. "This is a slice of heaven."

I release her hand and move behind her. She leans into my chest, and I wrap my hands around her as we both look out onto the scenery below. I agree with her, but the niggling in the back of my mind that the good must come with the bad keeps me from fully emerging myself in this experience with Nadia. I'm looking at the houses below, wondering how well we know the people. Are their homes littered with guns like mine?

Are they pretending to be decent people, or are they just decent criminals, if there is such a thing? I press another kiss to the top of Nadia's head.

"So, you want children?" I question and smile into the crown of her head as she tries to turn and look at me.

"Yes. One day."

I release her and let her turn so I can look down at her. "We could start now." I press a kiss to her smiling lips.

A fat raindrop lands on her forehead, and she looks skyward as warm rain starts to fall. She's still smiling as I release her, and she holds out her hands. "It's warm," she declares.

The rain falls steadier, and it reminds me of how heavy the downpours can be here in Spain.

She laughs, and I'm transported back in time to when we were just kids. When she looked at me in a similar way. We had been caught in the rain, and Nadia didn't want to go inside. She lived for each moment, just like now, as she opens her mouth and lets raindrops fall onto her tongue.

I capture her waist and drag her body to mine. My lips brush hers and it's like a sign. That we would be standing here, kissing in the rain all these years later, when that one moment had made me fall for her, and the aftermath destroyed me with my father.

"I love you," I say.

Her hands rest on my chest. She blinks the rain out of her eyes.

"I've always loved you."

Her gaze roams my face. I know she loves me, but she's holding back. She reaches up and touches my face.

I touch her cheek. "Why do you look so sad?" My chest tightens.

"I'm not. I'm so happy. But..."

She dips her head, and I capture her chin. "But..." I prompt.

"Nothing." She shakes her head.

"Tell me." I keep a finger under her chin. She blinks away more rain, and we're soaked through.

"It's just we wasted so much time. If I had known..."

I get what she's saying. If I had been more of a man and stood up to my father, we could have been together. If I hadn't stopped her from getting a job somewhere else, maybe her life would have been different. If her mother hadn't worked for us, I would have never met Nadia.

"We have the rest of our lives to catch up. We have forever, Nadia."

She nods and I release her chin. "I'm never letting you go again," I promise.

I press my mouth to hers, and I swear I taste salt on her lips. Recapturing her hand, I turn us back toward the villa. When we reach the green grass, Nadia starts to run back to the house, and I'm on her heels. She races up the stairs, and I love the chase. She reaches the veranda where we just ate, and I tighten my hold around her waist, pulling her to me. Her giggles cease as I turn her and capture her mouth with mine. My hand glides along her neck before I move lower and cup one of her breasts in my hand. I squeeze and she breathes heavily into my mouth.

"We need to get you out of those wet clothes," I say, scooping her up in my arms and carrying her into the villa. Water drips along the floor as I carry her to the bedroom. I kiss her at every opportunity until we reach the room. Placing her on her feet, I kick the door closed behind me and pull off my soaking shirt. Nadia tugs off her sweater, but it gets stuck on her head.

I smile as I walk to her and help her get it off. The wet top plops onto the floor as I walk toward Nadia, and she takes a step back, opening her trousers. She gets them down to her thighs, the fabric sticking to her flesh.

"Lie on the bed." She scoots onto the edge, and I pull off her boots, socks, and trousers. Her long legs part, and she leans back on her elbows. My cock throbs against my wet clothes, and I remove the rest of them as Nadia waits for me.

"Touch yourself," I demand.

She hesitates. I've never seen her hesitate before. She's unsure. "Touch yourself, Nadia," I growl.

Her hand slips under her panties and disappears out of sight, but I can see her hand moving. "Not your clit. Put her fingers inside yourself."

As I direct her, I take my hardened cock in my hand and stroke. She's watching me as her hips rise, giving her fingers access to her pussy.

"Take off your panties." I want to see what she's doing.

She removes her hand and slips them off. I continue to jerk my cock while I watch her lie back on the bed and spread her legs for me, giving me a full view of her pussy. Her hand glides down her stomach and past the hump before she inserts a finger inside herself.

"Good girl." My cock throbs as I watch her. I want to fuck her hard, but I keep that want at bay as I watch her fingers come out slick with her juices before she slides it back in slowly.

Her flat stomach rises as she adds another finger inside herself. I release my cock and fall to the ground. Gripping her knees, I force her legs apart, and she removes her hand, ready to bring it back up, but I capture her wrist and lean in, placing her fingers in my mouth. Her sweet juices run along my tongue, and I lap it all up before going to the source and drinking.

She exhales loudly as I run my tongue along the swollen bud. She jerks on the bed as I enter her pussy, pushing my tongue as deep as it will go. My hands glide from her knees to her thighs, and I squeeze the supple flesh between my fingers while dragging her pussy closer to my face until I can't breathe. Fuck me! I could die this way. Eating her out has my cock pulsating. I come up for air before running my tongue along her clit. When I stand up again, Nadia glances up at me.

I take my cock in my hand, again, and give it a few painful strokes. Without prompting, Nadia rises and reaches out, taking my cock in her hand. My eyelids flutter closed at the contact, and when her small pink tongue flicks out and licks the top of my cock, I fight for control. She uses her hand, and her mouth follows; she doesn't swallow my cock completely, and I'd love to let her take her time, but I need release.

Reaching down, I touch her ripe pussy, and she releases my cock. She lies back, both of us seeming to want the same thing. With my cock in my hand, I place it at her entrance, and I hope when my seed fills her, that her stomach will start to grow. That life will blossom inside Nadia. That my child growing in her womb will make her completely mine. *Until death do we part*, I think as I drive my cock into her tightening pussy.

She cries out and throws her head to the side. I fuck her like a man possessed, and the more she cries out, the harder I plow into her.

Grabbing her hips, I drag her closer until I can't get any deeper inside her. Nadia's eyes widen as I fill her completely. The walls of her pussy tighten around my cock, and she cries out as she comes. She's still rocking her hips as I lose myself in fucking her. Each slam brings me closer to coming, and when my seed finally pours inside her, I make sure to drive it as hard as I can so she will have my child. I'm still slamming into her even when I've come. I slow my motions and lean over Nadia, touching her stomach.

"I want my child inside you."

Her nostrils flare, but she nods. I fucking love her.

I press a kiss to her open mouth before extracting my cock from her.

She rolls onto her side, dragging her legs together and curling into a fetal position. "I want that, too." Her admission makes me a very happy man. I lie behind her and kiss her shoulder.

"What about a shower?" I ask.

She laughs. "Soon. Just let me lie here for a minute. They say it increases your chances of getting pregnant."

I smile into her shoulder. "Then we shall stay here forever."

She laughs and I press a kiss to her neck.

I'd lie here with her for eternity if that's what it took.

CHAPTER THIRTY

ALEX

FOUR DAYS PASS TOO quickly. The time with Nadia was a taste of the future. A future I now crave. The plane touches down on Irish soil. We're back. Back to a very stark reality. I have to tell my brothers I want out. I wasn't lying to Nadia when I said I could walk away, but I'm not sure how they will take it.

Nadia's hand rests on my lap. "I can be with you when you tell them."

"Thank you." I lean across and plant a kiss on her forehead. "But it will be fine. I'll do it when you go visit your mother."

Nadia had a lengthy conversation with her mother on the phone in Spain. It's one thing telling someone over the phone why you left your fiancé at the altar, and it's another to face her mother and explain why she didn't go through with the marriage.

In hindsight. Nadia was right. If she had married me, and the idea of losing her wasn't real, I don't think I would have ever walked away from this life.

The seat belt sign lights up, allowing us to get out of our seats. A limo outside brings us back to the house. My plan was to let Edmond take Nadia to see her mother while I called a family meeting, but it's not looking like I need to do that. I see Jason's and Aidan's cars in the drive.

"What are they doing here?" I say. An unsettled feeling rests on my shoulders.

"Maybe a welcome home party?" Nadia chews her lip. "Or a witch hunt for leaving you at the altar." Her joke isn't welcomed. A fierce protectiveness has me turning to Nadia. "My family wouldn't hurt you."

"I'm joking." Is she? I'm not so sure.

"No one would ever hurt you," I reinforce and Nadia nods.

"I'm going to get Edmond to take you to see your mother."

The limo stops at the door. "I can stay with you, Alex. We are engaged and should be doing this stuff together." Her intentions are lovely, but she has no place at a meeting like this.

"No, go see your mother, and it will be done when you get back." I lean across and place a kiss on her lips.

"Okay." She doesn't look sure, but I wouldn't have her at the meeting if it went wrong.

Jake is waiting in the hallway. "Your family is here in the drawing room." He doesn't sound happy. Jake's gaze dances to Nadia; his reason for not saying more.

"Can you get Edmond to take Nadia to the hospital straight away?" I say, putting an emphasis on the straight away part. I want her to leave as quickly as she arrived.

"No problem. I'll get on that." Jake leaves.

Nadia's hand slips into mine. "Best of luck."

I glance down at her. This is for her. No, correction—this is for us. My gaze travels further down to her stomach. Maybe for more than just us. That's what gives me strength. "I don't need luck. I have you."

I release her hand and place a final kiss on her forehead before entering the drawing room. Everyone is here and that makes me very fucking nervous. But I bury the nerves and open my suit jacket. "A welcome home party?"

"Aidan has called court," Jason growls from his stance at the fireplace.

I take a look at William and Matty, who sit on the couch. Matty is on his phone, and William salutes me with two fingers.

"Are you going to keep us all in suspense?" I ask Aidan, who looks tense. Whatever this is about, Aidan wouldn't call court lightly, and why couldn't this wait? It must be important.

"I was waiting for you." Aidan's solemn expression has me spreading my hands.

"I'm here now, so go ahead."

"I think the Russians killed Father," Aidan starts.

"And why would you think that?" Jason asks while sitting down on one of the armchairs. He rests his elbows on his knees. He appears relaxed.

I have no worries about this. Blaming the Russians would suit me just fine.

"There was a clause in Father's will: If Gilly and Jason died, everything returned to Alex." Aidan looks at us all. "Isn't that right, Jason?"

Jason sits back. "How the fuck would I know? I've never seen his will."

"Why would Father have a clause like that?" William says. "Maybe I'm fucking thick, but Alex has everything anyway."

Matty is no longer on his device. Instead, he's paying attention to what's unfolding. I don't like the road I think Aidan's about to go down, but I sit on an armchair and watch this play out.

"Because he didn't want it in Jason's or Gilly's name, so if they died, it would return to the rightful heir, Alex," Aidan continues.

Jason looks stung, and I don't blame him. He's really letting Jason know he isn't one of us. He's angry. Aidan isn't spiteful, but his actions are driven with anger.

"The rightful heir has his fucking throne," Jason barks. The cracks are starting to show.

"Okay, let's run with Aidan's theory, that in Father's will there is this clause. And you think because of that, the Russian's killed Father? I think if they were to kill anyone, it would be Alex. Wouldn't they want one of their own in power?" Matty turns to Jason. "No insult there, brother. But what you're saying, Aidan, doesn't make sense. Having Father killed wouldn't affect the clause." Matty's reasoning is sound, but Aidan is already shaking his head.

"I haven't figured it all out. But..." He glances at Jason, and pain fills my brothers' eyes. "You're Russian. You are so deep with them that you must know." Aidan takes a step toward Jason. "You're having secret meetings, doing their errands." Aidan's voice drops to a temperature that would freeze water. "You found out about the clause and lashed out at Father, killing him."

Jason stands up, and my brothers are toe to toe. "Why? Because he wasn't my fucking father which you love to remind me of?" Jason's hands slam into Aidan's chest, and we all move at once.

William and Matty are behind Aidan, while I feel obliged to defend Jason, as Aidan is so fucking out of line right now.

"What are you doing with the Russians?" Aiden asks.

Jason pauses; it's brief but noticeable. "I'm their negotiator."

I'm looking at Jason. He just lied.

"You lied," I say out loud, not meaning to.

"What is this, string up the fuckup of the family?"

I'm shaking my head. "That's not what this is."

Jason glares at Aidan, who hasn't backed down. "It feels like it."

"Did you kill our father?" Aidan's words are loaded with so much emotion.

"Fuck you!" Jason shouts in his face.

William reaches for Aidan, expecting Aidan to attack, but he doesn't. "Why? Was it because he didn't love you like he loved us?"

"Aidan, that's enough," I say. "Everyone, take a step back."

My brothers are slow to follow my orders, but they do—all but Jason.

"You said the Russians killed Father?" I remind Aidan, trying to get us back on track.

Aidan points a finger at Jason. "He's Russian. He fucking works for them. Has secret meetings with Kira's uncle. That's not how their hierarchy works. Isn't Kira's uncle an outcast? Thrown from his own throne by his brother?"

We all look at Jason. "You don't know what you're talking about." Jason exhales.

"Jason, you might be the negotiator, but your loyalty lies with your family," I remind him.

He's conflicted and my stomach hollows.

"What were the meetings about? Why did you kill the man Alex wanted to meet with? Fucking tell us!" Aidan roars, and William grabs Aidan's shoulders again.

I'm back to looking at Jason. "Did you kill Greg?" I ask.

Jason turns away from me and runs his hands down his face.

Matty breaks formation and spins Jason around, gripping him by his jacket. "Answer us." Matty is quiet. He's not volatile, but he can see what Aidan sees, what I now see. Jason is hiding something from us.

"Yes, I killed him. Now take your fucking hands off me." Jason calmly extracts Matty's hands from him, and Matty takes a step back, falling into line beside me.

"I fucked up." The wall of pretense falls, and I see a desperate man in front of me.

"What did you do?" William snaps, letting go of Aidan, who wears a look of satisfaction. A look that says, *I told all you motherfuckers so.*

"Kira's uncle was threatening her," Jason starts. "He asked for one small thing, or so I thought."

"I'm going to kill you!" William snaps and launches himself at Jason. They hit the ground hard. "You killed our father." His fist connects with the side of Jason's head, and I have a fear-filled moment thinking how that could be me.

I snap out of it and drag William off Jason with the help of Aidan. William's bulk makes him a two-man job.

Jason wipes blood off his mouth and gets up. He doesn't lash out at William. He's calmer.

"You fucking bastard!" William roars while Aidan and I hold him back.

"What are you shouting for?" Jason asks with a sneer on his face that curls into a growl. "I didn't hurt your father, so fucking stop."

Jason's words have William calming down slightly. William pushes Aidan and me away from him and walks in slow circles.

"If you would let me finish, I can tell you what I did." Jason holds his head high. He's about to own his shit, and I have great respect for that.

"He asked me for the location of a shipment as a form of payment. So I gave him the location of one of ours. That was the deal, and he would leave Kira alone. He told me I could blame Lexi, and it would all go away, as Lexi was going to clean the goods for them." Jason looks at each of us. "We wouldn't miss the money, and Kira would be safe."

I tilt my head. Jason isn't fucking stupid. "When did giving someone money ever solve a problem?" The only way to solve a problem in our world is to kill so they can't retaliate from beyond the grave.

"I couldn't kill him, Alex. He's too powerful. I hadn't known he would drop the shipment, along with the O'Reagan's shipment, for the Gardaí to find. I didn't know he was trying to remove us."

"So that's why the Russians were there at Lexi's. They were protecting their investment." Matty says.

Jason nods. "They had orders to take the kill shot if Lexi got too mouthy."

"Yet, they left," I remind Jason.

He nods. "Everything he told me was a lie."

"And now we're supposed to believe you?" Aidan asks and shakes his head.

"Yes, because he plans to wipe the Irish Mafia off the map, and the power behind him makes that possible."

"No, having a fucking turncoat like you makes that possible," Aidan barks, and William is coming closer. They want blood. They want their vengeance. I don't blame them. How stupid was Jason?

"You should have told us. We could have helped to protect Kira," I say. A part of me understands. I'm here to give all this up for Nadia. What bad fucking timing.

"Not from him," Jason admits and he wears the look of a defeated man.

"How do we know he's telling the truth?" Matty asks with a look of suspicion in his gaze. "I mean, he's a fucking rat."

"You all have short memories. We've all done bad shit that got us into a heap of trouble." I look to Aidan, thinking about him killing Gilly and the chain of events it caused. Or me killing my father, which sent us on a path of destruction and darkness, and it's not ending anytime soon.

"I'm fucking sorry, Alex, but maybe the Spanish weather fucked with your head. Maybe there's little men in between your ears clicking castanets. He is helping to wipe us out!" William claps his hands several times with temper. "So this isn't some *bad shit*." He's huffing.

Jason smirks. "You just can't stand me," he informs William.

"When I was with you, I nearly fucking died. You just have a knack for fucking things up." William's angry words make Jason flinch.

"Everything was fine until Father died. You had a hand in it. I just know it."

"I didn't kill him, you piece of shit," Jason retaliates.

He's launched himself at William, and they get into a fistfight on the ground. William gets the upper hand and dominates Jason. But Jason's anger has him bucking. Jason freezes as William puts a gun to his temple. We all freeze. Even the air freezes.

"Admit what you did! You took him from us!" William roars into Jason's face, pressing the gun harder.

"William, stop," I order.

William shakes his head. "This fucker has to pay."

"William, put down that gun now," I order again.

"I didn't do it." Jason is roaring, half-crying. "I'm your fucking brother." So much pain is forced into his words that it pierces something inside me.

"William, get off him." Aidan finally steps in. I'm expecting William to do as Aidan says, but instead, he pushes the barrel of the gun into Jason's temple.

The first wave of real fear washes over me as I think he's going to do it, and then everything I've done was for nothing.

"Kira is pregnant. Don't fucking do this," Jason pleads. He must see the madness in William's eyes.

"William, he didn't do it," I say.

"How the fuck do you know?" William roars, not looking away from Jason.

"Because I did," I admit.

CHAPTER THIRTY-ONE

ALEX

"**I** DID IT," I repeat, as William still hasn't let go of Jason.

My heart hammers in my chest, but my words slowly drag William off Jason. I'm watching the gun that hangs loosely between William's fingers.

"What?" Adain's brows drag together in complete confusion.

"You're just saying that to protect him," William accuses, but I don't know what he sees on my face because his words aren't so sure.

"Father gambled our fortune away with no care about it. He handed shares over to Frank like it was counterfeit money. He wasn't a good man." There, I've fucking said it.

But I can see no one agrees, not even Jason, who's gotten to his feet. His gaze tracks the gun William still holds.

"He put that clause in the will so everything would return to me when he had his men kill Gilly and Jason."

Jason pales, and I can imagine how this truth hurts. He did love our father, and now to hear the betrayal in such a way has to be hard.

"How do you know this?" William asks.

"Put away the gun," I order.

"Why should he? You just admitted to killing Father. Tell me you're lying." The end of Aidan's sentence sounds like a plea.

"I killed him, Aidan. He ordered me to kill Gilly and Jason. I couldn't do that."

Matty sits down, clearly overwhelmed with all this.

"You have been helping me…" Aidan's brows drag together. "You sat in your study with me. You discussed who could have killed him. You even allowed me to look at Jason."

"I couldn't tell you the truth, and I knew Jason was innocent," I tell him. William still holds the gun now tightly in his fingers. "I never wanted this. But I did what we were trained to do. If I didn't kill Jason and Gilly, someone else would. So I eliminated the problem."

"What the fuck is wrong with you? You're talking about our father!" Aidan shouts. "What if it was one of us?"

"But it was, and I protected him." I point at Jason, who looks like he's carrying the weight of the world on his shoulders. His gaze shines with unfallen tears. "He's our brother. I couldn't have him killed." I look to each of them, my own pain rising to the top. "I would have killed for any of you."

William runs his hand across the crown of his head with the gun I'm still watching. "Fuck's sake! This is so fucked up."

I don't answer. I'm grateful I'm still standing.

"Can I go now?" Matty asks, subdued.

"Are you serious? He just admitted to killing Father," Aidan reminds him.

I didn't expect Aidan to be standing at my shoulder, but I didn't think he would want blood. That's exactly how it's looking, though. My fear was mostly William. He's pacing now, and when I look to Jason, his gaze still glistens, and he's overloaded. I can't think of another word for it.

My emotions still haven't fully kicked in, and I wish I could feel the full impact of this moment like Jason is experiencing.

"What do we do, Aidan? Kill him? Kill Jason?" Matty shrugs. "We aren't a family. We haven't been for a long time." Matty walks to the door, but I can't let him leave like this.

"The court hasn't ended."

He sneers at me; it's cruel and filled with so much hurt that Matty won't let anyone see. "What are you going to do, Alex? Kill me? Make it look like a suicide?"

My stomach curls at his words. "Of course not," I respond.

"You all think I have one foot off the cliff, so let me be very fucking clear. You ever find me hanging from a ceiling or overdosed with pills, you can look at our mighty brother Alex." Matty leaves and slams the door behind him.

A punch in the face would have been easier.

"I found him," William says as tears leak from his eyes. "I found him hanging in his office. It fucking destroyed me." Veins bulge along his neck, and his face reddens. "That moment—finding him, wondering if he had clawed at his neck, if he had screamed and changed his mind at the last second…" William walks to me. "Wondering why I wasn't enough." William taps the gun to my chest. "You sick fuck."

"I had no choice," I respond.

William's laughter is tinged with hysteria. "Wow. You could have left him lying on the ground where you killed him. You didn't have to string him fucking up!"

"Did you kill Rob?" William laughs again. "Don't answer that. Of course you fucking did."

Aidan glares at me with a mask of devastation.

"Take the gun out of my face," I order William, standing up to him. I won't be prey. I won't be weak. I won't be ashamed of killing Father. I'm sorry I've hurt my brothers, most of all William. He wasn't meant to find

Father; I was. But he turned up at his office and beat me to it. It should never have been William.

"Killing you is too fucking good." William smirks and puts the gun away. "You have to live with what you have done."

"I know," I answer. "But we have bigger problems than me right now. We have the Russian mob trying to wipe us out."

"Let them wipe us out." William laughs.

"What do you suggest we do?" Aidan asks, but his gaze is loaded with hate.

I look at Jason. I'm a shovel for him to dig us out of this mess. "Tell us everything about them."

"He has an army. Men are arriving from Russia weekly. He never needed the shipment or money. It was just a ploy. He has everything he needs, and if the Gardaí don't do their job, then he will step in."

"So we're fucked." William claps his hands together. This is all too much for him. Him finding Father really messed with his head.

"We can start over," I suggest.

All gazes land on me. I keep going. "I was coming home to tell you I'm stepping down and moving to Spain."

William claps his hands, the sound as loud as a gunshot. "Well now, isn't that just convenient. When a war is starting, you're leaving for Spain." He's smiling bitterly while shaking his head. "My fucking God, you are good." William walks away and turns, pointing a finger at me. "You're a fucking coward."

"That's one thing I'm not. I did the job that needed to be done."

William nods. "You might have, but you didn't have to string him up."

"What do you want from me, William? Blood? I can't change what I did," I fire back.

"You could show some fucking remorse," William says.

I laugh for the first time. "Remorse?" I take a step toward him, my own calm taking a battering, the glass cracking. "We fucking murder people. Hmm, where is the remorse there? Don't be a hypocrite. It doesn't suit you."

"All hail our mighty leader, running off with his tail tucked between his legs," William mocks. "Your own woman left you at the altar because she knows what a fucking monster you are." The blow is too low, the air ripped from my lungs. I can take a beating on my character and actions. But not Nadia. That I can't bear.

"You mention her name again, and I will hurt you." My threat is low. I don't want to have to carry through on it, but I will.

William shakes his head. "I'm so done with this shit." He goes to walk away, but unfortunately, he can't. Having Aidan lead would be wise, but I need to give William all the power so he can have the full backing of the O'Rourkes when they go to war against the Russians. This is a time they need to stand together.

"You can't leave. You're taking my place."

Aidan and Jason both wear the same look of shock. I don't blame them.

William pauses his gaze full of suspicion. "Why? Why bypass Aidan? I'm sure I would be the last on your list."

"Because you're marrying Dillion O'Rourke's daughter, and you need to unite both clans to stand up against the Russians.

"What do you mean?" Aidan asks.

"I think there should be one Mafia. I think it's time to change the divide between the North, South, East, and West. I think if we all come together and work as one unit, nothing can break us."

"You keep saying 'us,' yet aren't you leaving?" Jason speaks up, his emotional state returning to normal.

"I think you need to get Kira and leave too."

He's shaking his head.

"That's an order, Jason. Think of your child. You will do more harm than good when this war comes. But right now, you are a valuable weapon to them. They will go to any lengths to keep you, including hurting Kira."

Jason closes his eyes; he knows I'm right.

"He's right, Jason," Aidan agrees, but I can still see the hurt in his eyes that I had bypassed him as leader, yet Aidan is bright enough to understand why.

"So you and Jason are leaving," William pipes up. "You give me the throne with no soldiers and a war on our streets."

I get William's fear, but behind his excessive nature is a leader. If he homed in on it, he could be unstoppable. I walk to my brother and grip the back of his neck.

"You have an army, but yes, the throne is yours, brother. I know if you really want to, you can turn this all around, William. You can save our family's legacy. Matty can't. Jason can't." I grip his neck and pull him toward me. "The reason you can is because you have nothing to lose. I have Nadia. I gave her my word I'd leave, or she will leave me."

"What about Aidan?" William's gaze is so troubled.

"It has to be you," I whisper, and I regret the decision I have to make. I've damaged William so much. I never meant to. "I'm sorry, brother." I pull him close until our foreheads touch. "I'm sorry about Father." *I'm sorry for what you witnessed.*

William's eyes fill with unshed tears, and he growls, pushing me away from him. Our moment is gone. I look to Jason and Aidan.

"I'll leave," Jason says, and I feel a slight weight off my shoulders.

Aidan still looks hurt, but it will pass. "I will back William one hundred percent."

I nod. "Then it's settled. William Murphy, the ruler of the West of Ireland."

William walks away from me again. I know this is all too much on them.

Jason is watching me, and I have one more question for him.

"When I was away at a meeting, a man tried to kill Nadia. He held her at gunpoint, and I killed him. He was part of the Russian mob. Did you know?"

"I swear to God, this is the first I'm hearing of this." Jason walks to me. "I know I've lied, but I've come clean, just like you. I would never allow them to hurt someone we love."

I nod. He's telling the truth. But that leaves either the O'Hanlons or the O'Rourkes who tried to kill Nadia. Both options tear us apart, so I can only believe it was the Russians who wanted to cause a divide. I would one day find out who sent that man to kill Nadia. But I know that's not today.

"Is court over?" William asks.

"Is it?" It's up to him now.

His bitter smile twists his lips. "Yeah, I think we have all heard enough for today."

William leaves, and I want time with Aidan, but it's like he knows. "I can't be around you right now."

I understand, so I say nothing as Aidan leaves.

"You're going to Spain?" Jason asks as he slumps down on the couch.

"Yes. You can pick a different country." I'm still pissed with the mess he caused, and I don't want my brother at my back door while I try to build a home for Nadia and me.

To think we would be scattered and broken isn't how I saw this going. But with William leading and Matty and Aidan backing him, they could win this.

For now, I would let sleeping dogs lie with the man who tried to kill Nadia. But one day, I would have my revenge. Right now. I would start living my life.

"Goodbye, brother," Jason says as I walk to the door.

I don't turn around but pause, my fingers tightening around the doorknob. "Goodbye, Jason."

I open the door and walk out into the hall. Once Nadia returned from the hospital, I would put everything into place and start over with Nadia and hopefully a new life.

A new legacy.

EPILOGUE

NADIA

"**L**ET ME PUSH YOU, Mam." I roll my eyes as she puts on the brakes of the wheelchair.

"I can walk, Nadia." She's so determined. She grips the sides of the wheelchair as she hoists herself out and stands. Once she's on her feet for a few seconds, she glances at me with a smile in her eyes.

She faces forward and takes a step toward the dining room table, where Alex rises to his feet. I walk carefully beside her in case she tires. It's been three weeks since her kidney transplant, and her recovery is remarkable. But I don't want her to overwork herself, either.

Alex pulls out a chair, and he's ready to help my mother into her seat.

"Thank you." She's fond of Alex, and they share a bond I didn't think would be possible.

Once she's settled, I take my seat beside her. "This looks delicious." Plates of salad and thick bread are being served for the afternoon tea. Life in Spain is peaceful, and the ebb and flow of time moves differently for us than it did in Ireland.

"The doctor said you're doing great," Alex informs my mother.

She looks so healthy, and I couldn't be happier. She loves life in Spain; afternoon siesta and warm evenings are doing wonders for her.

"I feel great, Alex. I really do. I've even started playing bridge again."

The staff mostly speak Spanish, but card games are truly universal, and they play for hours with Mam.

"I've heard the staff talk about it." A smile in Alex's eyes drips down to his mouth. When he looks at me, his smile expands, along with my heart.

I never dreamed I would love him more today than I did yesterday, but I do.

It's been three months of blissful peace in Spain. He really left the Mafia for me, but he says each night when I thank him that he did it for himself, too. I know he worries about his brothers. He left William in charge—not something I would do, but I don't fully understand all the politics behind his decision. He hasn't spoken to them, as he says they aren't ready yet.

One day, I hope they will come and visit us here. I'd love for Alex to have the unity of his brothers without getting involved with the Mafia again.

That's a fear that will never leave, him rejoining the Mafia.

I cut a slice of ham and dip it into the coleslaw. The tomatoes are a nice combination, and the juice from them runs across my fork. I want to sigh as all the flavors burst onto my tongue. Food here is so fresh, as we started to grow our own out back.

At first, Alex wasn't completely on board, but eventually he gave in and had an elaborate greenhouse built.

"I'm thinking I might like to see the beach." My mother drags me out of my thoughts.

I raise both brows. "You don't have to yet." She hasn't ventured outside the villa. She's starting to get stronger and a bit braver with each day.

"No, I want to." She's determined.

Alex smiles. "After food, we can go."

He's too good to us.

I take a drink of water, and I can't help but watch Alex. His white T-shirt makes his tan stark. He's taken to the Spanish weather like a duck to water.

I'm still burning, my skin slightly red if I don't plaster myself in sunblock. It's a small price to pay for the constant heat.

"We could pack a picnic for later," I add.

My mother smiles at me. "That sounds perfect."

I reach out and take her hand in mine. I've never been happier. This is perfect, this life we've built.

Alex takes a drink of his wine, and his gaze glistens with happiness as he watches me. His eyes dip to my stomach.

"Would you like some wine?" he asks.

"Water is fine." My stomach tumbles.

"Is the wine not to your liking?" he prods.

We are told not to announce a pregnancy until you have reached three months. But I can see the hope in Alex's eyes, and with my mother here, I don't think there could be a better time.

"No, wine isn't good for the baby." My free hand drops to my stomach.

Alex's face pales, but he shouldn't look so shocked. We have been trying ever since we got here.

"Baby?" My mother sounds breathless.

"You are going to be a grandmother."

Love, joy, and every emotion pour from her. Her hand shakes as she pulls me into an embrace. "Oh, a little Nadia running around."

My throat and nose tighten, and I swallow the emotion. I've been overly emotional lately, and when I took the test, it confirmed why. I'm pregnant. Just four weeks. "It's early. I'm a month along."

My mother breaks the embrace, and I get to look at Alex.

His hands rest on the table, and he's slumped back in his chair. "I'm going to be a father?" Emotions well but don't spill over.

I nod. "And I will be a mother." That thought is a little terrifying, but with my mother and Alex being here, that fear dissolves.

Alex gets out of his chair and walks to me. I'm ready to stand when he falls to knees and pushes my chair away from the table. His hands instantly go to my stomach.

"You can't feel the baby move yet." I'm trying to laugh as he presses his ear to my stomach. I glance at my mother, and she smiles with joy.

"I bet it's a boy," Alex says with his ear and hands still pressed to my stomach.

"Is this what I will have to endure for nine months?" I ask.

Alex looks up at me. "Every day." He presses a kiss to my stomach.

I think I could get used to that. His hands leave my stomach, and he takes my face gently.

"You've made me such a happy man. The first time by being with me, and now you are giving me a child." He leans up and presses his lips to mine. "Thank you." He sounds so grateful, and he shouldn't be.

But I don't say all the things I want to, as I can see this has far more depth than I understand right now.

"I wonder if you will be thanking me during the night feedings and dirty diapers." I try to make light of the situation.

Alex smiles and hooks his arm as if he's holding a baby. "I can't wait."

I wonder what I did to deserve a man like Alex. He rises and pushes me back in with a sigh of bliss. He returns to his seat, and the conversation stays on the baby.

It's a new beginning.

It's an end to the old. I take my mother's hand.

It's a second chance for us. For all of us.

Have you read the O'Reagans yet? You can start with Mafia Prince HERE

About Vi Carter

When Vi Carter isn't writing contemporary & dark romance books, that feature the mafia, are filled with suspense, and take you on a fast paced ride, you can find her reading her favorite authors, baking, taking photos or watching Netflix.

Married with three children, Vi divides her time between motherhood and all the other hats she wears as an Author.

She has declared herself a coffee & chocolate addict! Do not judge Social Media Links for Vi Carter

Website

Facebook Reading Group

Facebook Author Page

9 781915 878199